CHAPTER ONE, MURDER

"Dammit, George!" exploded Mr. Chapman. "Why the devil did you have to tell me that you suspect this may be a true story?"

Mr. Meredith's lip curled in ironic amusement. What could be more exasperating to a publisher than to be told in one breath that he had been offered a potential bestseller and in the next that it might be inadvisable to print it?

"Libel can be very expensive," Meredith said calmly. "Not to mention the undesirable publicity."

"You're probably right," he muttered, as he untied the string that held the manuscript sheets together. Mr. Chapman turned over some pages of *A Most Mysterious Death* and read a sentence here and there.

"Is it really so very good?" he asked wistfully.

"Very good indeed," was the uncompromising reply. "A new *Jane Eyre*. The governess-narrator, the dark, mysteriously fascinating employer and the mad wife."

"And one of them is murdered? Which one?"

"The wife, naturally."

"And which of them is the perpetrator of the crime?"

"I leave you to discover that for yourself . . . ."

THE LADY IN BLACK

ANNA CLARKE

BERKLEY BOOKS, NEW YORK

This Berkley book contains the complete text
of the original edition. It has been
completely reset in a typeface designed
for easy reading and was printed from new film.

THE LADY IN BLACK

A Berkley Book / published by arrangement with the author

PRINTING HISTORY
William Collins Sons & Co., Ltd., edition published 1977
Berkley edition / July 1990

ISBN: 0-425-12168-2

A BERKLEY BOOK® TM 757,375
Berkley Books are published by The Berkley Publishing Group,
200 Madison Avenue, New York, New York 10016.
The name ''BERKLEY'' and the ''B'' logo
are trademarks belonging to Berkley Publishing Corporation.

PRINTED IN THE UNITED STATES OF AMERICA

10 9 8 7 6 5 4 3 2 1

Contents

Author's Note

Apart from George Meredith and Frederic Chapman and their respective households, all the characters in this book are entirely fictitious. (As a matter of fact, I have invented Mrs. Chapman because I can't find out anything about her; the establishment at Banstead is documented, however.)

Quotations from Meredith's *Modern Love* are taken from the edition with an introduction by C. Day Lewis, published by Rupert Hart-Davis 1948; and quotations from *Diana of the Crossways* are taken from the Mickleham edition, Constable 1922.

1

A Mysterious Caller

At about two o'clock on Thursday afternoon, the first of May in the year eighteen-hundred-and-eighty-two, a tall young woman, dressed in black and closely veiled, was making her way through the crowded streets round Covent Garden market in a southerly direction. Under her arm she carried a large brown paper parcel, and every now and then she shifted its position and clutched it to her bosom, as if it were some precious treasure that she feared might be stolen from her. As she picked her way through the cabbage stalks and rotten apples that strewed the paving stones where the market produce had been unloaded, she thought of the young newspaper reporter who had trodden these very stones more than fifty years ago, on his way to purchase a copy of the magazine in which had been printed the very first story he had ever written. There would never be another Charles Dickens, of course, but even he had once been young and apprehensive and unsure of his own gifts.

Not that she herself had any wish to become so famous. In fact, it was extremely important that her own name should never appear on anything she wrote. She stopped on the corner of Henrietta Street, once more clutched the parcel to her bosom, and drew a deep breath. It was madness to go on; it had been madness to write it down at all, but it had been such a relief to put it into words, and once begun, there had been no stopping. The joy of composition was like no other joy on earth; the power that she wielded with her pen had gone to her head like wine. And the fact that it had all had to be done so secretly, without anyone in the house suspecting that she was writing anything at all, only added to the excitement, for she was no coward, and was at her best when challenged by danger and difficulty. Particularly when to that spice of risk was added the sweetness of love. Did she still love him? She could not tell. Even the writing of this novel had not enabled her to answer that question. All it seemed to have done was to shift her passion on to the novel itself, her very own child, not another's.

A market cart rattled by over the cobblestones, the driver shouting at his horse. Three young clerks, returning from lunch at an inn to one of the neighbouring offices, jostled each other on the pavement, laughing at each other, talking loudly together, friendly and boisterous as puppies. They gave her a curious glance as they came near, stepped into the mud of the roadway to avoid pushing past her, and walked on rather more soberly than before. She did look like a widow, she supposed, dressed like this, but it had seemed the best way to avoid being recognized, and after all, there had been a death, and she might well be mourning it still.

She moved a few yards along Henrietta Street, telling herself that she could always say she did not want the book published after all. In any case it was very unlikely that any publisher would be interested in it. Young ladies all over the country were for ever writing poetry and novels: why should anybody consider hers to be better than other people's? Thus she reasoned with herself. She wanted an expert opinion, that was all; she wanted a literary adviser to tell her straight out that her book was feeble and undistinguished and that there was no possibility of her ever writing anything that was not. That would settle it once and for all. She would have tried her best, and failed; honour and pride would be satisfied, and at the same time she would be saved from taking a most foolish and dangerous step.

But in her heart she knew that she did not want this at all. She was in love with her own writing, and she craved for somebody else to love and admire it too.

Just to admire it. That would be enough. Not to print it. If by some miracle any suggestion of actually publishing her story were to be made, then she would make some excuse, say she had changed her mind and was not offering it for publication after all.

Having come to this resolution she felt strong enough to walk along Henrietta Street and pause near the archway that led to the Church of St Paul's, Covent Garden. That would be the office, just opposite. A low step led to a big brown door, flanked on the right by a pilaster with a Corinthian decoration at the head, and on the left by a rather dingy looking window. But there over the window were the magic words—CHAPMAN AND HALL—the firm who had published Charles Dickens and other great names too. It was disappointing, in a way, that their offices did not look more imposing. On the other hand, it was the very drabness of the place that gave her the courage to enter.

A dark and steep staircase led both up and down; a glass door labelled "Enquiries" was to her left. There was an odd smell about the building. She lifted her veil for a moment and sniffed. Strong cheese, was it? No, it was game. Pheasant or grouse or something of that sort, and very high too. It must be coming from the market, not from the publishing house. Her imagination was playing her tricks, and no wonder, after all the events of the past two years, which had been enough to unsettle even the toughest mind.

She pulled the veil over her face again and opened the door marked "Enquiries." It was no use dithering about like this: she had made up her mind and she was going to do it. A bright-looking, rosy-cheeked lad of about fifteen years of age, who had been poring over a desk, got down from his high stool and came towards her.

"Good afternoon, ma'am. Can I help you?"

He spoke with a slight stammer. He seemed to be even more nervous than she was, and he was looking around as if hoping that someone would come out of the rabbit warren of offices, of which she had caught a glimpse through the inner door, and help him to deal with the visitor.

"Yes," she said, drawing herself to her full height and speaking in her firmest and most dignified voice. "I believe you can. I have with me the manuscript of a novel that a friend of mine has written. She is desirous of obtaining an opinion as to its merits."

"Oh yes, ma'am, indeed, ma'am," cried the boy. "Is this it? May I take it from you? Thank you, ma'am."

The brown paper parcel was yielded up and placed on the high desk at which the boy had been seated. An awkward silence followed. It was clear that something more ought to be said, but neither knew quite what to say. The boy glanced at the door in the partition that led to the other offices, hoping to see one of the older clerks come in; the visitor glanced round the room and thought how dirty the desks and shelves were, and how untidy the floor, with piles of books and bits of packing paper lying around. It needed a woman to clean the place up. A good, competent housekeeper, with a couple of sturdy young women working under her, would soon have the place in order.

The thought of housekeeping brought to mind the smell of game that she had noticed in the passage. She mentioned it to the boy. He pounced on her remark eagerly, glad to find a subject on which he could safely converse.

"Oh yes, ma'am, it is game indeed, a whole haunch of venison. It's been downstairs where the books are packed for ever such a long time now and the packers say it's terrible, the smell of it."

"But why do you have a haunch of venison in a publishing office?"

The lady was plainly both puzzled and amused. The boy could see her lips, just visible beneath the veil, part in a smile. "It's Mr. Frederic's ma'am, Mr. Frederic Chapman, our Managing Director, that is. He's a great sportsman and he likes game. Got a whole larder of it downstairs, he has, and a cellar too. A wine-cellar, I mean."

"Good gracious! I never heard of such a thing. What a strange man he must be."

"Oh yes, ma'am, he is. He's a real character, a real old sport. But he don't like slackers. He's got a little window, back of his office upstairs, and he can see most of us on the ground floor from there. You should just hear him if he thinks somebody isn't working hard enough!" The boy's eyes opened wide in wonderment. "Never heard such language. Roaring the place down, he was. But he's a capital fellow, all the same. And very kind if anyone was to be in any trouble, they say."

"They say?" The visitor was quick to see the implication of these words. "You have not been working very long with the firm, then?"

"No, ma'am. Only started this week. There's ever such a lot to learn, but I know I shall like it."

"I'm sure there must be, and I am sure you will do it very well indeed." She was full of gracious condescension now. After all her hesitations and her fears, to find nothing more alarming than a very raw recruit of an office boy was a great relief. Did that not prove, yet once more, that if you screwed up your courage and took the plunge, the difficulties would melt away and you could achieve things that you had never dreamed of?

"Will Mr. Frederic Chapman read my friend's novel?" she asked.

"I—I don't rightly know, ma'am," said the boy, suddenly shy and stammering again.

"Does he not read any of the manuscripts that are offered to you?"

"Oh yes, ma'am. That is to say, I believe he does."

"But not always, perhaps? Who else will read it?"

"I think perhaps it will go to Mr.—to our reader,
ma'am."

"And who is your reader?"

The boy looked even more embarrassed, blushed, and
murmured: "I can't say, ma'am."

"I hope he is a man of discretion and discrimination,"
said the visitor, with some severity.

"Oh yes, oh yes indeed, ma'am. Of very great discrimination indeed. If you will excuse me now, ma'am."

The boy climbed back on to his high stool and began
to unwrap the parcel. At that moment the door of the room
burst open and in rushed a stout little middle-aged man in
spectacles, wearing a dark suit with two buttons missing
at the bottom of the waistcoat.

"What's this, what's this? Who is this lady, Tom?" he
exclaimed, creating instantly a great impression of bustle
and activity in the office.

"She has brought a manuscript, Mr. Goodbody." Tom
indicated the half-unwrapped parcel. "And I was just going to—"

"Yes, yes," The stout man interrupted him impatiently,
and then turned to the visitor. "Delighted to be of service
to you, madam, very happy to give our most earnest consideration to the work with which you have entrusted us.
You have been given a receipt for it, I believe?"

The visitor turned her head to Tom, who said a trifle
defensively: "I was just going to write it out, Mr. Goodbody."

"That's right, my boy. And the address too. We shall
require the address for communication."

"Yes, sir."

Tom began to write, with Mr. Goodbody fussing behind
him and trying unsuccessfully to peer over his shoulder.

"Now mind you write clearly. You'll get nowhere as a clerk in this business if you do not write a good, clear hand."

"Yes, Mr. Goodbody."

"Have you asked the lady her name?"

"Not yet, sir."

Mr. Goodbody turned to the visitor and spread out his arms in an expansive gesture of deprecation.

"You must excuse me, madam, for not being present to attend to your request myself, but I was at that moment urgently required by our Managing Director, Mr. Frederick Chapman."

"I quite understand," said the lady in black. "I have been very well entertained by your deputy in your absence."

She smiled at the boy Tom, who blushed again, while the older clerk frowned at him and shook his head.

"To whom should I make out the receipt, ma'am?" asked Tom.

"To the name on the manuscript," was the reply.

"It says, 'by Faith Freeman' on the title page."

"Then make it out to Faith Freeman," said Mr. Goodbody testily. "Make haste, my boy, make haste. You must do better than this if you are to suit Mr. Chapman's requirements."

Breathing heavily, his face only a few inches away from the sloping top of his desk, Tom wrote in a beautiful copybook hand:

"Received the manuscript of a novel entitled *A Most Mysterious Death* by Faith Freeman, dated this First Day of May in the Year Eighteen-hundred-and-Eighty-two."

He looked up: "Please may I have your address, ma'am?"

"Oh." The visitor pondered a moment. "My friend wishes to remain anonymous and I myself shall be travelling for a while. It would be best, perhaps, if you were to address correspondence to Miss Faith Freeman at St. Martin's-le-Grand.''

Tom looked up at Mr. Goodbody. "Is that all right, sir?"

"Certainly, certainly, if that is what is desired. Write it down. Do you know how to spell it?"

"No, sir."

The older clerk took the pen from the boy's hand and wrote.

"That is the main Post Office in all London, in all the country," he explained. "When you send letters for people to collect from there you must put on the envelope 'Poste Restante.' Like this." He wrote the words. "That's French. There you are, my lad. You have learnt something new today."

He was quite genial now, glad to show off his authority in front of this somewhat mysterious, but very dignified and self-possessed visitor.

"When may I expect to hear from you?" she asked.

"In two or three weeks' time, madam. Our reader will be coming in today. There are always a great many manuscripts for his perusal, of course, but I may, if I am lucky, 'catch the Speaker's—or rather, the Reader's—eye' on this occasion."

Whenever a manuscript was delivered by a lady or gentleman in person, Mr. Goodbody produced this little joke. It created a good impression, and gave them the feeling that the firm had their interests at heart. The personal touch, he called it; let them feel that they are singled out for special treatment. Of course the manuscript would probably turn out to be rubbish, as ninety per cent of them were, but one never knew. The next one might always be the very one that was not rubbish at all. You never could tell. That was the great thing about working in a firm of publishers—you never could tell. Mr. Goodbody lived in the constant hope of one day being able to tell his grandchildren and great-grandchildren that he had been the first, the very first, to welcome some new Charles Dickens or Anthony Trollope across the threshold of the firm. You never could tell.

The lady in black was ushered to the door and bade goodbye, after she had politely declined the suggestion that a cab should be summoned for her.

"Now, my lad," said Mr. Goodbody, returning to the office, "you have done very well for a first time. Never forget this. Whoever the caller is, you never can tell. This lady now—what did you take her for?"

"A young—yes, I think she was young—a young widow in deep mourning and not wanting to let her grief be seen," said Tom.

"Right. Quite right. A young gentlewoman, we ought perhaps to say. And yet who knows? In a year's time her name may be a household word as an authoress."

"But she said it was her friend—"

"Aha!" Mr. Goodbody shook his head, wagged a finger, and looked very knowing. "You must not take any notice of that. They all say that it has been written by a friend. No, my boy, that novel is the lady's very own work, or my name is not James Herbert Goodbody. And her name is not Faith Freeman either. I wonder what it really is? Very anxious to remain anonymous, is our fair young author. *A Most Mysterious Death*." He picked up the big bundle of neatly handwritten sheets. "And a most mysterious lady, to my way of thinking. A most mysterious lady."

2

Enter a Poet

The lady in black lingered for a few moments on the pavement outside the offices of Messrs. Chapman and Hall, Publishers, looking across the road towards the archway that led to St. Paul's Church. She had a sudden impulse to go into the church and kneel down and say . . . well, what should she say? A thanksgiving or a confession? The trouble was that she really did not know. She had made her confession, if one could call it that, in the oddest possible way. It was lying even now in the offices of Chapman and Hall, awaiting the judgement of their reader. As for a thanksgiving, she was not at all sure about that either. In a way, she supposed, she had obtained her heart's desire, but somehow it did not seem to be what she really wanted after all.

But still she hesitated, staring at the paving stones. It had taken all her strength and courage to hold her poise during the last half-hour, and the need to give way and unburden herself to somebody was very strong. There was no human creature to whom she dared tell the truth: perhaps it would help her a little if she were to kneel down and whisper it to her Maker.

A light clatter of horse's hoofs drew her attention, and she looked up to see a hansom cab stopping only a few yards away, and a goodlooking gentleman of about fifty getting out of it. He was a striking figure, dressed in a frock coat and a scarlet tie, and his thick springy hair and short beard were iron-grey.

He glanced at her as he came towards the doorway in which she had been standing. Averting her head, and pulling her veil further down over her face, she went hastily on her way. There was something rather disconcerting about the keen look that the gentleman had given her, not because he appeared to be the kind of man against whom a handsome lone woman would need to protect herself, but because he looked so very shrewd and intelligent, the possessor of a mind that would penetrate all disguises and ruthlessly expose the truth.

Could this be the great Mr. Chapman, she wondered, the roaring sportsman who kept wine and venison in the cellar, who swore at his staff when they were lazy, and of whom they seemed to be very much in awe? She rather thought not. Such a man as the office boy had described would surely not look so crisp and neat. Besides, this gentleman did not look as if he would roar and swear. Quiet, deadly sarcasm, perhaps; that would be more in his style. And had not that silly pompous old clerk, Mr. Goodbody, said that he himself had just come from attending on Mr. Frederic Chapman, in which case the Managing Director could hardly be arriving a few minutes later in a hansom cab?

She went on her way, pondering, and the man who had got out of the cab stood looking after her. Who could she be? What was her business at Chapman and Hall? There was something hauntingly familiar to him about that tall figure and about the full generous mouth and firmly-moulded chin that he had glimpsed under the veil. The hair seemed to be black, too. He frowned, shook his head, and muttered something to himself.

Of course he knew her. But not in the way that the majority of people would understand. He knew her better than any living creature had ever known another; only God could know man as he knew this beautiful woman, with her fine figure and her dignified bearing, so at odds with the rather fearful and secretive air that she wore. He knew her because she was his own creation, his glorious, witty, unfortunate Diana, who had possessed his mind and heart for many months past and who would not let him rest until the last word of her story had been put on paper by his own pen and in his own hand.

And perhaps not even then, for the characters in his novels never left him. Once they had taken hold of his imagination they were his companions for ever. His heroines in particular were in a sense more real to him than even his beloved wife Marie, or his "dearie girl", their daughter Mariette. He was always, half-consciously, looking for his characters, as if somewhere, outside his own imagination, they must exist. A retreating figure, a face seen for a moment in a crowd, even an old portrait, would bring him tantalizing glimpses of his own creatures in the flesh; and then they were gone, and lived once more only in his mind.

The black-clad figure turned the corner out of view, and the gentleman from the cab gripped his cane and his case more firmly and stiffened himself and looked about him, once more seeing only the dirty windows and the drab street. His Diana must wait until the peace of the evening. There was a home and family to provide for, and even poets sometimes had to eat. For this hard cash was needed, and Chapman and Hall paid hard cash, though not very much of it.

He opened the "Enquiries" door, gave a mock salute, and called out cheerfully: "Greetings to all poor London-grimed toilers on this bright May morn."

The three clerks—for a dark, serious-looking young man had joined Tom and Mr. Goodbody—looked up from their desks and smiled. They did not know that they were looking at the comic mask of a poet; they did not even think, at that moment, that they were in the presence of a great writer at all. They only knew that a bit of sunshine had come into the dull routine of their working lives.

Mr. Goodbody got up from his stool.

"Good afternoon, Mr. Meredith, sir," he said.

"Afternoon, Jamie lad. And you, Peter Piper." Thus had the dark young clerk been christened when it became known that he was learning to play the flute. "And here's a new smiling face to brighten up our darkness," continued the newcomer.

"Tom Stiles, Mr. Meredith. He joined the staff this week."

"How do you do, Mr. Stiles?" The great man shook hands solemnly with the blushing boy. Then he added, in lighter tones: "And what ambition brings you here, pray? What gilded future do you see beckoning to you from beyond these dusty portals?"

"I want to learn the trade, sir," said Tom, looking a trifle bewildered.

"The trade? Good. You would like to be a publisher? Or a bookseller perhaps?"

"That's right, sir."

"You do not, I trust, have secret yearnings for literary fame? You do not wish to become a writer?"

"Oh no, sir. I could never be a writer. I am not hoping for that, sir."

"You are wise, Tom. It is a dog's life. A cringing, squalling, hangdog sort of a life. Nothing but kicks while you live and all the glory when you're dead. What use is glory when you are dead? Who wants glory when they are dead? Tell me that, pray, Peter Piper."

"I suppose," said the dark young man with a smile, "that the Salvationists would say they want glory when they are dead."

"Ha! I like that. But we want neither harps nor laurel wreaths, do we, Tom? We want our fair share of the goods of this earth below. May some of them be yours one day.

Ah well. To work. You have received the parcel of manuscripts? Good. Here is the register.''

He replaced on Mr. Goodbody's desk the big ledger, bound in red morocco, that he had been holding under his arm, and continued: "The verdicts are therein. Nothing of interest at all this week. All the fools in Christendom appear to be converging on Chapman and Hall with their empty vessels. Not a drop of the precious liquid in any of them. Not one of them has even the first tadpole-wriggling of an idea.''

"Oh dear, that is a pity, Mr. Meredith," said Mr. Goodbody. "Mr. Chapman will be very disappointed.''

"No more than I. Dross, dross, dross, and never a glitter of gold. What have you put aside for me next?''

"Six novels, I believe, Mr. Meredith. Or perhaps seven. A lady has just brought one in this afternoon.''

"A lady? Clothed all in black?''

"Yes, sir.''

"She brought a manuscript?''

"Yes, Mr. Meredith. Here it is. But I could leave it over for next week if it is too much for you now.''

"Pack it up with the others.'' He thought a moment. "No, I will take it with me now. Parcel it up again, will you, Tom, while I go to do my duty upstairs. Is Mr. Chapman in?''

"Yes, sir.'' Mr. Goodbody paused a moment, and then said, tentatively: "Did you notice when you came in how strongly the venison is beginning to smell?''

"Did I notice? My dear fellow, I did my best not to notice, but my endeavours were unsuccessful. Oh that the offending beast could be removed to Banstead and to Mrs. Chapman's cook!''

"That is just it, sir.'' The packers are complaining that it is quite dreadful downstairs, and makes them feel all faint in the packing room, they say, what with the gaslight and the smell of rotting game. Well, what we wondered was whether you might very kindly drop a hint to Mr.

Frederic that he might take it home to Banstead and eat it now. Have a quiet word with him, as it were.''

"The word shall be spoken, James." Mr. Meredith waved a hand and left the room. The door had scarcely closed behind him when Mr. Goodbody and Peter Piper, whose real name was Peter Bond, grabbed the red morocco-bound ledger, opened it, and began to pore over it together. A moment later three more clerks appeared from the inner offices and joined them, all jostling each other to get a better view.

"What has he said?"

"Any good ones this week?"

"There ought to be if the manuscripts were all rotten."

The new boy, Tom, puzzled by this activity and wondering what was going on, came near too, but failed to catch a sight of the ledger with all the others crowding round it.

"Stand back, stand back," said Mr. Goodbody. "I will read it to you if I find anything—ah, here we are." He began to chuckle.

" 'Feebler stuff than this might be written,' " he read aloud, " 'but would tax an ape.' "

The other clerks laughed.

"That's one for you, madam poet," said one of them. "What does he say about that Donkey book?"

"The Autobiography of a Donkey?" Mr. Goodbody placed his finger on the title as he read the reader's verdict aloud:

" 'Faithful only to the donkey's business.' "

"Asking for that, the author was," said another of the newcomers. "Oh, I like this one! 'Apparently by a muddle-headed beginner, bothered by the expression of his views and ideas.' "

" 'An infernal romance,' " read out Mr. Goodbody, snatching the register back again. " 'Wild weak stuff— manuscript looks like the survivor of a dozen shipwrecks.' "

"That must be the one we had to put together with sticking plaster," said Peter Bond. "What do they think we are here? A doctor's surgery?"

Tom, who had been hovering on the edge of the group, looking rather puzzled, now found the courage to interrupt the older clerks and ask what they were talking about. Mr. Goodbody answered him with his usual condescension.

"This, my boy, is the register in which all the manuscripts that are offered to Chapman and Hall are entered."

He picked up the red ledger and showed it to Tom.

"On the left is the date, then come the title and name of the author, and here on the right you will see a wide space left for Mr. Meredith's comments on the book to be recorded. Mark it well, Thomas Stiles. This is an historic document. The day will come when someone will be proud to own it."

Tom was impressed. He had been inclined to mark Mr. Goodbody down as a pompous and self-satisfied old blighter, for in spite of the boy's shyness and unfortunate tendency to blush, he had a mind of his own. This time, however, he felt inclined to trust the older man's judgement, particularly as Peter Bond, who seemed a sensible sort of person, was nodding in agreement. But something was still worrying him.

"Isn't Mr. Meredith a writer himself?" he asked.

"Yes, Tom," said Peter.

"Then why is he so unkind about these other writers? He would not like anyone to say such unkind things about him."

The clerks looked somewhat taken aback at this remark. It was a new thought to them. They were neither better nor worse than the great majority of men. They did a long day's work for a small wage, and when they left the office they returned to humble homes with squalling children and tired wives. Mr. Meredith's visits were the brightest spot in their working week. He brought them a little glimpse of a world beyond their own, a world where words made magic. They could not have put it into words themselves, and half the time they did not even understand what he was saying, but a little core of romance deep in their hearts recognized it and responded. Besides, he never spoke sarcastically to the clerks and would always stand up for them in any dispute, for "what am I myself," he was fond of saying, "but a hardworking hack of a cabhorse?" His manuscript register was always good for a laugh: surely they might be permitted a few moments away from their desks to relieve the tedium of the slow-moving hours?

Tom sensed that he had not been understood, and hastened to try to explain himself.

"I hope he won't say anything unkind about that lady who came in with the book just now," he said breathlessly. "She was a friendly lady and she talked to me. I don't want her to be made unhappy."

It was Peter Bond who was the first to grasp what was troubling the boy.

"She will not see it if he does," he said quietly. "None of the authors ever see any of these comments about them. If the book is bad they are told that it is not suitable for our list, or something like that. Nothing more. They are disappointed, of course, but they are not hurt. Not really hurt."

"Oh I see." Tom looked greatly relieved. "But doesn't Mr. Meredith ever say a book is good?"

The men laughed again and one of those who had come in from an inner office said: "Of course he does, you nincompoop. Otherwise we would not be in business. This is a publishing house. We have got to publish something. We do not live on air."

Peter, seeing the boy go scarlet at this remark, took it upon himself to explain further.

"If Mr. Meredith likes a book," he said, "he will say so in the register and tell Mr. Chapman. And then Mr. Chapman will read it, and perhaps another of the directors too. And if Mr. Meredith thinks the book is not very good but that the author may perhaps write a better one some day, he tells us to write and say so. And if he thinks the book needs altering before it is published, then we write to the author and invite him to meet our reader, who will give advice about revision. There are two people booked for this very afternoon. Most weeks there is somebody who needs some help, and once, they say, for that was before my time, there was a young man Mr. Meredith was so excited about that he talked to him for hours about his writing and would not pay any attention to anything else. He had the same name as yours. Thomas, Thomas Hardy. So you see we are not such unkind people after all, Tom, and if your friendly lady has written a very silly book, she will not be told so. Not by us, at any rate."

"I do not believe she has written a silly book," said Tom firmly. "I believe she has written a good book that needs changing a little, and that means she will have to come in to the office to talk about it, and then I shall see her again."

"Hark at the champion of damsels!" exclaimed the somewhat uncouth clerk who had laughed at Tom before. But this time the boy did not mind. He felt that Mr. Peter Bond was his friend; he had learnt quite a bit about the job and had a glimpse into the great world of literature; and as he climbed back on to his high stool to write out the list of addresses that Mr. Goodbody had told him to, his heart and the best part of his mind were busy weaving their own private romance about the beautiful and mysterious lady in black.

3

If Only We Could Find a Best-Seller!

Upstairs, in the big front room on the first floor that was still called Mr. Chapman's room, although in fact since the firm had become a limited company it had been officially designated the board-room, a rather less light-hearted conversation was taking place. Mr. Frederic Chapman, a burly man with a big beard, was indeed very much a sportsman, as much at home with a gun in his hand as with a manuscript. He had been with the firm for many years, and commanded the respect and loyalty of both staff and authors. But perhaps he was beginning to grow a little weary of the business sometimes, and to dream of retirement. At any rate, he looked very glum when Mr. Meredith flung himself down on a chair and exclaimed: "Rotten bunch again this week, Fred."

"And last, and the next week too, I suppose. What is happening to all the good authors nowadays?"

Mr. Meredith shrugged. "I wish I could find them. I am sorry that I am not able to manufacture such creatures. There is a certain proverb about a silk purse and a sow's ear. If we had but the sow we could at least breed from her, but all that comes our way is the pigswill."

"What we need," said Mr. Chapman broodingly, "is another Charles Dickens."

This was so obvious a desire, and at the same time one

so hopeless of fulfillment, that Mr. Meredith did not trouble to reply.

"If only," began Mr. Chapman, and then paused.

His companion tensed himself. The two men were old friends and colleagues and had many tastes in common, including a love of outdoor life and of books on natural history and travel and exploration. For nearly all the time they worked in perfect harmony together, but just occasionally a slight coolness arose. It rather looked as if one might be coming up now.

"If you are regretting that we did not publish *East Lynne*," said Mr. Meredith stiffly, "I can only say that nothing on earth will ever cause me to revise my opinion of that book, not if it sells in millions until the end of the century. It was and it remains a foul book, pandering to the very lowest elements of the most degraded popular taste."

Mr. Chapman hastened to reassure his friend that he had not been thinking of this "foul" book that had been rejected some years back by Mr. Meredith, only to make a fortune for a less discriminating publisher.

"No, no," he said, "we backed your judgement on that. We always do rely on your judgement, George. We have a high reputation to maintain and we do not wish to become known as peddlers of trashy novels. But the fact remains that we have too few promising young authors on our list, and we cannot live on Charles Dickens for ever. I was only going to remark that if you could only—"

He broke off again. He was very far from being a cowardly sort of person. But many another strong man had hesitated before venturing to lay himself open to the biting lash of George Meredith's tongue.

"It is a great pity," he said at last, "that so many people find it so difficult to understand your own novels."

The man sitting opposite him scarcely moved, but it was as if his whole body had suddenly turned to steel. "I am what I am," he said coldly, "and I write what I write."

"Yes, my dear George." Mr. Chapman was very placatory now. "You have received so much praise from greater minds than mine that you can hardly wish me to add my own poor little quota. But when it is a matter of appealing to a wide popular readership—if without compromising your great gifts in any way you could make it just a little bit easier for people to understand you—"

Yet once more he broke off in the middle of a sentence. The absurdity of seeming to suggest that his friend should devote his talents to writing penny dreadfuls or cheap romances had suddenly struck him with full force. It was like asking Robert Browning to compose little verses for mass production on Christmas cards. Authors were the touchiest fellows in the world, as who should know better than himself, and he would never have dreamed of making such a suggestion if he had not been really worried. This was no way to run a successful business. He waited stoically for the icy blast to hit him, but this time it failed to blow.

"I am here in the capacity of literary adviser," said Mr. Meredith, still cooly but without malice, "and as such I discharge my duties to the best of my ability."

"Yes, my dear fellow, of course you do."

The awkward moment was over, leaving Mr. Chapman relieved but still not happy. George was a wonderfully brainy fellow, of course, and no doubt scholars would still be arguing about his writings years after most of the popular writers of the day had been forgotten, but it was often the stupider people who made the money. If only he would try for once to suffer fools gladly. Or perhaps not exactly gladly, for that would be asking too much, but at least try not to annihilate them. Mr. Frederic Chapman sighed inwardly, while outwardly he composed himself to discuss the essential business of the firm for the next half-hour. At the end of that time Mr. Meredith rose to his feet and said he had appointments to keep.

"Miss Olive Schreiner, I believe, will be an acquisi-

tion,'' he said, "and I have a strange stirring of a notion—
I really cannot tell you why—that something else of interest to us will materialize before too long. And by the way,
Fred:'' he paused at the door. "Talking of sows—what
about that stinking carcass of venison that you are har-
bouring downstairs? Could this be the reason why the authors are staying away? Has the word gone round? Wend
not thy way to Chapman and Hall or the curse of the skunk
will upon thee fall. Can't you use it for one of your gabble-
gobble dinner parties? Take it away soon, that's a good
chap—man.''

"All right, George. I will get the boy to put it on the
cab when I go.''

Frederic Chapman could not help feeling, as those who
talked with George Meredith so often did feel, that he had
had rather the worst of the exchange, but he vented his
feelings later that afternoon on the unfortunate Tom. The
boy had understood Mr. Chapman to say that the venison
was to be placed in the four-wheeler cab, but when Mr.
Chapman entered the vehicle and found himself with a
most offensive fellow passenger on the seat, he got out
again and let loose the full flood of his invective. The
terrified boy gathered that the carcass should have been
placed on the roof, and he decided, when he went home
to his widowed mother that evening, that he did not like
publishing after all, and if it was not for the hope of seeing
the mysterious lady in black again, he really believed that
he would tell his mother he would like to look for another
opening.

While this little drama was taking place in Covent Garden, Mr. Meredith was getting out of the train at the small
country station near Box Hill and gratefully filling his lungs
with the sweet downland air. Swinging his cane in one
hand and in the other the briefcase containing, among other
papers, the manuscript brought by the lady in black, he
strode along at a great pace towards Flint Cottage. The
small, square house was almost hidden from the road by

high box hedges; a dachshund came barking down the drive towards him, and Mr. Meredith put down his case in order to greet the dog.

"And a very good welcome to you too, Jacob," he said, amongst the frantic lickings and leapings. "What's the score of rabbits today? Coming up for the century, eh?"

He moved on, and in the intervals of the dog's barking there were to be heard the beautiful cool strains of a Chopin nocturne coming from the open window of the small sitting-room. Mrs. Meredith was an accomplished pianist, and Chopin her favourite composer. She left the little upright piano, however, as soon as she heard the sounds of her husband's arrival. George was very fond of music, but not at all fond of a day's business in London. He was a bundle of nerves at the best of times, and if the day had gone badly he would be more tense and irritable than ever. It was best to keep the house quite quiet and make only the most noncommittal remarks until she saw how the land lay. She did not mind putting her own feelings in the background. She was a Frenchwoman, perhaps rather an old-fashioned one. She believed in the sanctity of the home and the duties of a wife; she was devoted to her children and cared for her difficult and temperamental husband with great tact and skill. She knew that whatever he said—and he could be bitterly unkind in speech here at home too—in his heart she meant everything to him, and that was enough.

This day could not, at any rate, have been a particularly bad one. He greeted her and the children with absent-minded affection and was very distrait during dinner, not hearing what was said to him, and sometimes murmuring inaudibly to himself. There was nothing unusual in this, no cause for alarm. It only meant that his restless, relentlessly active mind was busy churning words over and over, feeling their rhythm, testing the way they slipped together. After dinner he would go up to the wooden chalet at the top of the steep orchard garden behind the house, and write and write. There were two little rooms in it, one a study and the other a small bedroom with a hammock bed. If the ideas were flowing very fast he would stay there all night, writing for many hours and then sleeping for one or two, but at dawn he would be up again to take long strides up to the top of Box Hill to watch the sun rise. That was the way he was, and she accepted it. If he wanted to tell her something or ask her advice, he would do so when the time came.

On this particular evening Marie Meredith was correct in all her suppositions except one: George did not, at first, write and write. His *Diana* was waiting and some dimly-felt verses were hovering at the back of his mind. Yet he resolutely put pen and notebooks aside and sat down to study the manuscript that had been handed to the office boy by the mysterious lady in black.

The first impression was very favourable, on account of its physical appearance alone. Twenty years as a publisher's reader had added to Mr. Meredith's strong natural cynicism a very large quota of the disillusionment customary among members of that trade. The sheer, blind, thoughtless vanity of so many aspiring authors had at first amazed him, but now he was prepared for anything: for totally illegible handwriting; for manuscripts written on both sides of paper so thin that it was impossible to see which words were on which side; for manuscripts that were a puzzle maze of corrections and arrows and rings and insertions; manuscripts that had become so battered by their journeys in and out of every publisher's office in London that they fell to pieces in your hands yet still the ever-hopeful author sent them on; manuscripts with the pages out of order, manuscripts with some of the pages upside down, and so on, *ad infinitum*. It seemed as if the authors were hell-bent on using every possible means they could to torment the very man on whom the fate of their brain children depended.

Even when the clerks in the office had sifted through the scripts to the best of their ability, still plenty of horrors remained. Shakespeare himself would have received a jaundiced glance if presented in such a form. And when all these obstacles had been overcome, the pages put straight and the handwriting deciphered somehow, and the reader doing his best to overcome his annoyance with the author and to give him a fair reading, the result was so often yet another feeble imitation of a good writer, or a raw, undigested lump of experience quite obviously taken straight from the writer's life. Mr. Meredith gave every script as much attention as he felt it deserved, for in spite of his acid tongue and uncertain temper he was a conscientious man and his love of literature was deep and sincere. Besides, as James Goodbody was so fond of saying, you never could tell. Even in the most hopelessly messy and ill-written of the scripts there might lie the spark of genius whose discovery brought a thrill that was ample reward for all the tedium and the tired eyes and the frustrated mind.

A Most Mysterious Death by Faith Freeman was written in a strong, neat hand on good quality paper, with well-spaced lines, and wide margins. The paragraphs were indented, and the dialogue was easily identifiable as such. So, too, was the speaker. There was no question of having to look back to an earlier page, or count the number of speeches, to discover which one of the characters was uttering which words. Mr. Meredith gave a little grunt of relief and made a mental note: she contrives good dialogue. And to the mental note were very soon added others, equally complimentary: she draws her characters from life; she can drive and sustain a narrative.

Mr. Meredith read at great speed. How else could one turn over thousands of pages, take in the essence of millions of words, year after year? When he was about a quarter of the way through the book he stopped reading for a moment, blinked, and rubbed a hand over his eyes before looking at the page again.

"That's odd," he said to himself. "A mistake in the name of a character. I should not have expected her to make such a slip. She writes so carefully and consistently well. However, it is the first such error I have noticed and it is only a minor character."

But a few minutes later he came across a similar error; this time one of the chief characters in the story was designated by a different Christian name, not once, but several times. Not only that, but the handwriting was less neat and controlled than it had been up till now, as if the author had either written in great haste or had been labouring under strong emotion during the writing. It was, indeed, a particularly tense and gripping section of the story. The governess-cum-secretary who was narrating the tale had just declared her love for the man in whose household she was employed; it was a triumph of passion over conscience, because the gentleman in question already had a wife—albeit a hopeless invalid. It was a fine dramatic scene, which had been well prepared for in the preceding chapters, and it posed the big question: Will they or will they not yield to temptation? With the author's remarkable ability to convey the moment by moment fluctuations in mood of her characters and the subtle nuances of human thought and action when under the strain of great feeling, this big question promised a most interesting development of character and plot throughout the rest of the novel.

Mr. Meredith put the unread part of the manuscript down on the floor beside his chair and got up to stretch his legs. He took no more than a couple of turns around the two little rooms, however, before he was back again with *A Most Mysterious Death*. Not only was it very well written, but it was also an exceptionally gripping story. It was very rarely indeed that he managed to forget that he was reading as a duty and found himself racing away with a book reading for pleasure, but this was what was happening now. He noticed another couple of slips in a character's name similar to the one that had occurred in the big love scene, but by this time he was completely caught up in the story and did not stop to wonder about them. Only when he was nearing the end did his attention start to flag. He shifted restlessly in his chair and his fingers beat an impatient little tattoo on the pages remaining to be read.

"No, no, no, woman," he muttered to himself. "You cannot suddenly introduce at this stage a long-lost lover who has never been mentioned in the book before. That will not do at all."

He skimmed through the final chapters, continuing to mutter at intervals. "No, no. It won't do. This must be changed. No, madam, you cannot lead us so bravely all this way and then lose your nerve at the final fence. You do not lack courage. You must not shirk the ending. Kill him off, kill yourself, take the veil and become a nun, live on tormented by guilt—finish the book as you will so long as it be true—true and convincing as all the rest. Do this and you have written a fine book indeed."

At the last page he exclaimed aloud in disgust: "Canada! That too! Why do they always have to escape to Canada when they do not know how to end a novel? And she was doing so well up till then. A pity."

He bent down and picked up the pile of manuscript sheets from the floor and shuffled them together into a neat pile which he placed on the table. After that he sat and thought for a little while and then picked up the teak board which he used to support the paper when he did his own writing, propped it up on his knee, and dipped a quill pen into the blue ink. After reading through the paragraphs that he had written the previous evening he began to add to them.

"I suppose we women are taken to be the second thoughts of the Creator; human nature's fringes, mere finishing touches, not a part of the texture,'' said Diana . . . ''However, I fancy I perceive some tolerance growing in the minds of the dominant sex. Our old lawyer assures me the day will come when women will be encouraged to work at crafts and professions for their independence. That is the secret of the opinion of us at present—our dependency. Give us the means of independence, and we will gain it, and have a turn at judging you, my lords! . . . I am a married rebel, and thereof comes the social rebel . . . I was once a dancing and singing girl. You remember the night of the Dublin Ball?''

''You are as lovely as you were then,'' said Emma.

''I have unconquerable health, and I wish I could give you the half of it, dear,'' said Caroline . . .

Mr. Meredith suddenly gave a little start. The hand holding the quill pen shook and a drop of ink blurred the neat script of the last words written. I've done it again, he muttered to himself; whatever is the matter with me? He drew a line through the words ''said Caroline'' and wrote firmly: ''said Diana.''

A little later he wrote:

The Plaintiff in the suit involving her name was adjudged to have not proved his charge. Caroline heard it without a change of countenance . . .

Mr. Meredith laid down his pen and admonished himself for a minute or two before he once more corrected the character's name.

The following morning he asked Marie to pay particular attention to the names of the characters when she was making a fair copy of the fourteenth chapter of *Diana of the Crossways* for him.

''I believe I have several times written 'Caroline' instead of 'Diana'," he added. "Please check it for me, will you, my dear, and make the correction in the copy."

"Caroline," said Marie Meredith thoughtfully. "Why should you keep writing 'Caroline'?"

"I don't know," replied her husband. "I can only suppose that my mind is running on the woman who was the model for the character of Diana. I have based her on Mrs. Caroline Norton, you know. Sheridan's granddaughter. She was supposed to be Lord Melbourne's mistress when he was Prime Minister, and her husband brought a suit against him, and she was also Sidney Herbert's mistress. You must have heard the stories, Marie."

Mrs. Meredith had certainly heard the stories. "Are you not afraid that the character will be recognized," she asked, "and Mrs. Norton's friends and relatives take offence?"

"It may be advisable to make the usual disclaimers," said George, "stating that the story is to be read as fiction, but on no account should a mistake in the character's name appear in print. To say it would be unfortunate would be putting it mildly."

"Very mildly," agreed Marie with a smile. "The courts could make much of that in a libel case."

"There is no question of libel," said George, "but it might well cause distress and ill-feeling."

"I should be sad if it did that," said Marie, a trifle anxiously. "I wish you would be as careful of yourself and your reputation as you are of that of Chapman's authors. You always watch for possibly offensive matter when you are reading, do you not, George? It would be ironic indeed if you saved Frederic Chapman from such pitfalls only to drop into one yourself."

"No, no, my love, it is perfectly all right. I know what I am doing. If you would make quite sure that the character has the right name, that is all. It seems to be easy to make slips of the pen of this kind when our thoughts have been very concentrated on the living model for the fictional character. Good heavens!''

The last words had been exclaimed in quite a different tone of voice. Mr. Meredith jumped up suddenly from the table in the little sitting-room where Marie played the piano and did her writing and translating work, and without any word of explanation rushed out of the room. A moment later Marie saw him pass by the window and hurry up the steep path through the orchard garden towards the chalet at the top. She raised her eyebrows and gave a little shrug and settled down in a leisurely manner to her copying. Had it been anybody else behaving in this way she would have been concerned enough to find out whether they had noticed that the house was on fire or a cow got into the garden or some similar catastrophe; but since it was George, she simply assumed that he had been suddenly struck by an idea and could not wait to follow it through. She took up her pen and began to write:

As the day of her trial became more closely calculable, Diana's anticipated alarms receded with the deadening of her heart to meet the shock. She fancied she had put on proof-armour, unconscious that it was the turning of the inward flutterer to steel which supplied her cuirass and shield. The necessity to brave society, in the character of honest Defendant . . .

Marie Meredith pursed up her lips and gave a little unconscious shake of the head as she wrote. Her mind was not quite in sympathy with this latest heroine of George's who had deserted her husband and was accused of adultery; a woman in such a position ought to hide herself modestly away, instead of flaunting her beauty and her wit in the company of other men. Women who took it upon themselves to flout society in that way had only themselves to blame if they suffered for it. However, it was not her task at this stage to criticize, so she wrote steadily and carefully on.

Meanwhile Mr. Meredith, in a much greater agitation of mind than his wife, had picked up the manuscript of *A Most Mysterious Death* that lay on the desk in the chalet and was leafing through its pages. When he came to the chapter containing the big love scene he read it through carefully and then turned over more pages until he found the other places where a character had been given the wrong name. Then he rubbed a hand across his forehead and looked very thoughtful.

"Can it be possible?" he asked himself. "Could any author be so rash? To draw from the life of a real person in a case of adultery is one thing . . . but to use a living model when it is a case of murder! . . . Why, that could be equivalent to signing one's own death warrant. And yet, and yet . . ."

Mr. Meredith sat over the manuscript of *A Most Mysterious Death* for a long time, looking more and more worried.

4

Here Is Our Money-Spinner, BUT ...

"Dammit, George!" exploded Mr. Chapman, bringing his hand down heavily on the manuscript sheets that lay on the blotter. "Why the devil did you have to tell me that you suspect this may be a true story?"

Mr. Meredith's lip curled in ironic amusement. Poor old Fred. What could be more exasperating to a publisher than to be told in one breath that he had been offered a potential bestseller and in the next that it might be inadvisable to print it?

"Libel can be very expensive," he said calmly. "Not to mention the undesirable publicity."

Mr. Chapman gave his colleague a baleful look. He was always a little nervous about infringing the law, or offending against morality, as Mr. Meredith well knew.

"You are probably right," he muttered, as he untied the string that held the manuscript sheets together. "You usually are, damn you." Except when it is a question of pandering to the vulgar taste, he added, but not aloud, because this was not the moment to start arguing with George, who had, after all, taken the trouble to come into the office outside his usual hours. Mr. Chapman turned over some pages of *A Most Mysterious Death* and read a sentence here and there.

"Is it really so very good?" he asked wistfully.

"Very good indeed," was the uncompromising reply, "apart from the ending, which will have to be altered. A new *Jane Eyre*. Of similar power and intensity and a not dissimilar theme. The governness-narrator, the dark, mysteriously fascinating employer—a lawyer, by the way, at least in the story—and the mad wife. They are all there."

"And one of them is murdered? Which one?"

"The wife, naturally."

"And which of them is the perpetrator of the crime?" Mr. Chapman glanced up at his friend as he spoke.

"I leave you to discover that for yourself," replied Mr. Meredith. "Let me not spoil your pleasure. It is an exceedingly gripping narrative, I assure you."

"I will read it this evening," said Mr. Chapman, "and see whether I come to the same conclusions as yourself. These slips that you mention—could it not be that the author changed her mind about the names originally given to these characters but forgot to alter them when she made the fair copy of the book?"

"That does happen," admitted Mr. Meredith, "but it is curious that they should always occur at moments of great tension in the story and be accompanied by a marked deterioration in the handwriting and the general condition of the script. You will see what I mean. These pages have very much the appearance of pages taken from a private diary written under great strain—possibly great anxiety as well. And when you add to this the indisputable fact that I found myself repeatedly writing the Christian name of the lady on whom my own heroine was modelled instead of that with which I had endowed the character, and the equally indisputable fact that the author of *A Most Mysterious Death* is taking considerable pains to disguise her identity—a heavy veil, a pseudonym, an accommodation address—plus the fact that the novel is real and convincing far beyond the usual run of even quite praiseworthy fiction—well, you will understand that I felt in duty bound to inform you of my suspicions."

"Deuced decent of you, George, to look in to tell me about it," said Mr. Chapman with genuine gratitude. "I hope you have not come up to town specially on that account."

"By an earlier train, that is all," was the reply. "Marie has gone shopping and I am to meet her at John Morley's. We are to dine there and go on to the opera. *Die Entführung aus dem Serail*," he added in a perfect German accent that irritated Mr. Chapman, himself neither linguist nor scholar. But that was George all over, he said to himself. Just when you felt yourself warming to him because he was so utterly honest and trustworthy and altogether a thoroughly good fellow at heart, he would suddenly say something that made you feel terribly inferior and stupid, and infuriated you so much that you wanted to kick him.

Mr. Chapman took a grip on himself and returned to the business in hand. "You have almost convinced me already," he said, "even before I have read the book. And yet it seems incredible that any writer could be so indiscreet. Have you ever come across anything like this before?"

"Not in any manuscript worth serious consideration," admitted Mr. Meredith, "but since the suspicion first entered my mind this morning, I have been thinking about it a lot, and I do remember on one occasion skimming through one of those masterpieces of feebleness and banality in which a similar plot—if plot it can be called— was employed, and the murder of a spouse took place. I remember wondering at the time whether the wish had been father to the thought and thinking that if the author had no better facility in execution than he had in composition, he would be hard put to it to accomplish a successful murder. I say 'he' because the name on the title page was that of a man, but it was probably a pseudonym, as the name on this manuscript undoubtedly is. In this case, however, the author has not tried to disguise her sex, as so many women do. She has courage."

"To the point of foolhardiness, if you ask me," said Mr. Chapman, picking up the manuscript again and handling it in a rather gingerly manner, as if it were liable to get up and bite him.

"It is certainly a novel way of making a confession of murder," said Mr. Meredith. "Most unusual, but full of possibilities. The situation in itself would make an admirable basis for a story. A dozen plots could be devised, starting from this very conversation that we are now having."

Mr. Frederic Chapman noticed a threatening gleam in the other man's eye. "Yes, yes, no doubt," he said hastily. If George once became launched on the elaboration of a plot for a novel there was no knowing when he would stop. It was capital entertainment to listen to, of course. In fact, if only George would write down his stories as he told them, he would make a fortune for both himself and the firm. There had been one occasion, at a dinner in an hotel, when not only all the guests at table, but also those at the neighbouring tables and even the staff of the hotel, had stayed on long after the dining-room should have been cleared, held spellbound and laughing till they cried at George's fantastic tales. But this was not the moment for such harmless amusement.

"If we do not take this book," he said, "the author will offer it to another publisher."

"Very likely."

"Whose reader, lacking the excessive discernment and scrupulousness of yourself, will recommend its publication without a qualm."

"No doubt. He will also lay his firm open to the possibility of somewhat unpleasant consequences."

"Yes, yes, I know, and you know how grateful I am to you," said Mr. Chapman. "But it is the devil of a fix, all the same. Could you see the author, do you think, and wriggle the truth out of her somehow? If any man could get at the truth, you are the one."

"I suppose I shall have to see her," said Mr. Meredith without enthusiasm.

"And you can tell her that she must change the ending and make any other alterations that are necessary. You always do this sort of thing so much better than I do, old man," added Mr. Chapman a trifle anxiously.

"I will do my best," said Mr. Meredith, not sounding at all pleased. It was just like old Fred, he was thinking, to hand him the thankless task of telling an author to revise a manuscript. Some of them took it well and some of them did not, and in the latter case it could be a most wearisome and frustrating business. For a man who wished simply to carry out faithfully the work he was paid for and then get on with his own writing, it seemed to Mr. Meredith that he spent an extraordinary amount of time smoothing out internal dissensions in the firm, pacifying angry authors and customers, and generally acting as referee and peace-maker. Worst of all, Fred seemed to have been losing his grip rather of late, and getting himself into awkward situations, like promising to publish that monumentally tedious work of a prominent Anglican divine that would have involved the firm in great losses, and then leaving Mr. Meredith to get out of it by means of an exhausting theological argument and by a firm declaration of his own agnosticism which had fortunately sent the bishop scurrying off, deeply offended, to a less heathen publishing house.

Mr. Meredith could not help feeling that he was being increasingly put upon, but he could also not help putting his mind to whatever problem was before him, and so he said, after a moment's reflection: "I think the manuscript ought to be copied. Marie would do it, but she is busy copying for me and working on that translation. What of the clerks? Peter Bond is a quick and reliable writer. And discreet. He will keep quiet about it, I believe, though I would not trust Goodbody or any of the others."

Mr. Chapman showed some amusement at his friend's earnestness. "Why the rush, old fellow?" he asked. "Are you afraid that the lady is going to change her mind and burgle our offices to get the manuscript back?''

Mr. Meredith did not laugh. "Can you have that copy made and either keep it safely at home yourself or else give it to me to keep?'' he asked.

"Yes, yes, of course. Might be needed one day as evidence in a murder trial, eh? Young Peter in the box swearing that it is a true copy—George in the box stunning both judge and jury with his wit. Ha, ha, ha!''

Mr. Meredith listened resignedly while Mr. Chapman continued to exercise his humour in this manner for several minutes longer. It was a show of bravado, no more. Mr. Chapman was very seriously concerned about the book, and even more so when he put down the last page of the manuscript late that night, with an expression of distaste on his face. It really was a very horrid story, although so well written and so convincing, and it would no doubt sell like hot cakes.

He woke up his wife to tell her about it; he badly wanted to talk to somebody, not least to get the taste of the thing out of his mouth.

"I do not quite know what to do, my love,'' he said, after briefly explaining the situation. "If George thinks, after seeing the author, that the events recorded in the book are dangerously near to the truth, then I feel we have no option but to reject the manuscript. I can see no other course. We cannot possibly publish for all the world to read a true account of a presumably undetected murder.''

"But somebody else would publish it, not suspecting it to be true?''

"Undoubtedly.''

"And,'' continued Mrs. Chapman sleepily but doing her best to apply her wits to the matter, "the people concerned may read it and recognize themselves and take alarm, and possibly a fresh tragedy might come about. Is it not your duty to try to prevent such a tragedy?''

Mr. Chapman groaned. This was a new aspect of the situation.

"How?" he asked.

"Should you not take this manuscript to the police authorities and explain that you have reason to suspect that it is an account of a real crime and leave its investigation in their hands?"

"But we do not know for sure. It is only conjecture. The police would laugh at us, and if we were to set them on to completely innocent people—"

"If they are innocent they have nothing to fear, and if you are laughed at, well, laughter breaks no bones. And for all you know, a death may have taken place about which the police are already suspicious, and this story may be of great help to them in bringing the guilty person to justice."

"My love," said Frederic Chapman, greatly impressed, "I believe you are right. I have been looking at it purely from the viewpoint of a publisher. You have reminded me of my duty as a citizen."

"Did not Mr. Meredith point this out to you?"

"No, but he suggested that we should immediately make a copy of the manuscript and put it in a safe place."

"Then no doubt this was what he had in mind," said Mrs. Chapman, and after that she refused to discuss the matter any more and went resolutely back to sleep.

Her husband was unable to follow her to this refuge for another hour. Quite apart from his duty as a citizen and his problem as a publisher, the haunting horror of the story he had just read had taken a grip on his mind. It was so frighteningly convincing. He tossed about in bed, trying to fix his thoughts on something cheerful and agreeable like fishing or shooting rabbits, but always they came back to the account of the murder, and by the time he eventually fell asleep he was wishing with all his heart that he had never seen the beastly manuscript at all.

Peter Bond was delighted to be entrusted with an urgent and important job of copying that would bring him in some badly needed extra money. He had married the previous summer and a first child was on the way. His Lucy had been a governess and was a good musician. They were for the most part very happy, loving and making music together in their tiny cottage in Islington, though sometimes Lucy would refer rather wistfully to the beautiful pianos on which she had played and taught her pupils during the days when she had worked in the houses of the rich. It was Peter's great ambition to buy for her a better instrument than the battered one with which she had had to make do since their marriage. And the baby, of course, would involve a lot of expense.

Lucy, too, was pleased to hear about the copying work and offered to help. Peter had only a moment's qualm. He had been told that it was urgent and confidential but had not been told the reason why. Surely it could not be so confidential that his wife could not see it? And in any case, they had only the one tiny living-room, and it would be impossible for him to carry out the work at home without her knowledge. Together they would get it done at twice the speed—nay, more than twice, for she could work during the day when he was away at the office.

"Are you sure it will not be too much for you?" he asked.

Lucy laughed. Peter was a very fond and anxious father-to-be.

"I shall enjoy it," she said. "What is the book about?"

"A murder, Mr. Chapman says. Rather an unpleasant one."

"Ooh! That is good!" Lucy opened her eyes wide and gave a pretended little shiver of horror. "It will not be dull, then. You know I love to be frightened—in a nice safe way, of course. But if it is an exciting story, then we shall both of us want to read it all. How shall we split up the work?"

After a little discussion it was decided that Peter should start copying that evening and that the next day, when he was away at work, Lucy should check through what he had done before going on to copy the next chapters herself. Peter would check her work before he began again, and so on until the whole of the manuscript had been copied. In this way they would both of them have the pleasure of following the story as they worked.

The meal was cleared away; the crimson brocade curtains that had been Lucy's wedding-present from her last grateful employer, were drawn to shut out the remaining light of day; the lamp was set in the middle of the square mahogany table, whose shiny dark surface was always covered by a thick red cloth with tassels that hung down to the knees as one sat. Peter spread out his paper and pens and ink on one side of the table: Lucy took a seat opposite him and settled down to her sewing. For a long time there was no sound in the little room save the ticking of the clock on the mantelpiece, the occasional rustle of paper, and the faint scratching of Peter's pen.

When Lucy saw her husband yawn and rub his eyes she said firmly: "That is enough for tonight, dear. Is it interesting?"

Peter did not answer: he was turning over pages from the heap yet to be copied, blinking with weariness, but leaning over the manuscript as if he could not bear to let it go.

"It seems to be very interesting," said Lucy with a laugh, as she pulled the papers gently away from him. "I think perhaps I had better not read any of it tonight, or we shall neither of us have any sleep."

The thought that his Lucy might be deprived of her night's rest brought Peter back to reality. He rubbed his eyes again, shook his head, and placed the manuscript and the writing materials neatly on the sideboard.

"Well, he said, as he stretched out a hand to extinguish the lamp, "it is a strange story indeed. A strange gruesome story, I fear. In spite of her love of horrors, I am afraid it might distress my dearest Lucy."

His dearest Lucy laughed again and said that nothing of the sort ever upset her, that he knew what a glutton she was for that sort of thing, and that she could hardly bear to wait till tomorrow in order to enjoy the manuscript. In spite of these bold words, however, it was a serious and rather worried-looking Lucy who replied the following evening when her husband asked her how she had been progressing with the copying work.

"I have a dreadful confession to make, my dear," she said. "I have not done as much of the copying as I should have. I became so absorbed in the story that I could not bear to wait to know what happened, so I left off copying and read right through to the end."

"Never mind," he reassured her. "It still saves me some of the work."

"Oh, I will do some this evening. We will work together. I do not mind which chapters I copy now that I know how it ends."

"And how does it end, my love?"

"Do you really want me to tell you?"

"I do indeed." Peter had been looking at her closely. He was always quick to notice how other people felt, as Tom the office boy had learnt, even when these people were comparative strangers to him. He could not, therefore, fail to notice that Lucy was not at all her usual calm and cheerful and slightly domineering self. "It has upset you, after all, this story," he went on. "You will feel better about it if you tell me too."

"It has upset me," admitted Lucy, "but not only for the reasons you think."

"Come. Tell me."

"Aren't you very hungry?"

"I can wait a little longer. Tell me now."

Peter sank into the armchair near the window that looked out on to the little front garden. The sky was still light, the evening was warm. He was tired after his day's work and the long walk home, but the only thing that really mattered to him was to comfort Lucy. She pulled a low stool up to his chair and leaned against his knee. He shut his eyes and gently stroked her hair as he listened to her firm, clear, rather schoolmistressy voice telling the story.

5

A Lover of Horrors Is Greatly Disturbed

"It will be no surprise to you," said Lucy, "to hear that Mr. Henry Windlesham QC and Miss Julia Lovegrove fall deeply in love. They declare their guilty passion for each other on a balmy evening in late spring, just such as this evening, but in considerably more luxurious surroundings than those in which you and I, dearest Peter, are sitting so contentedly now. They are, in fact, in the conservatory at the rear of a large mansion in one of the fashionable squares in Kensington. The conservatory leads off from the room that Mr. Windlesham uses as a study, and where he not only keeps his law books and other sections of his library, but many of the curios and souvenirs that he has assembled during his journeyings in Africa and other exotic lands. Native spears and daggers, drums and other barbaric instruments, strange and colourful head-dresses and masks associated with the peculiar rituals and ceremonies carried out by these savage peoples. Mr. Windlesham has a great knowledge of such matters. Miss Julia takes an interest in them too."

"Naturally, if she loves him," said Peter lazily, still fondling Lucy's hair.

"She had no right to love him," said Lucy sharply. "He was another woman's husband—a poor, sickly, mad woman, with a pathetic little wisp of a daughter."

"You forget, my love, that this is only a story," said Peter.

45

Lucy took a deep breath. "Yes. I'm sorry," she said at last. "I must hasten on, or you will never have your meal. The poor crazy Laura Windlesham is lying in the back bedroom on the second floor, from which she seldom emerges. She has been moved there from the front room, because the sight of the trees in the Square gardens moving in the wind frightens her. She is full of fears, terrified of everything and of everybody. She has been like this for eight years, ever since the birth of little Hetty. The most eminent physicians have been consulted in vain. Opiates are prescribed, and complete rest and freedom from any excitement or exertion. There is nothing else to be done. Henry Windlesham has no wife—nothing but a pale, shivering ghost. Little Hetty has no mother, because Mrs. Windlesham can scarcely endure to see her. The child lives on the first floor, in the room under her mother's. A nursemaid sleeps in the room with her, for Hetty is very frightened to be alone. She is clever and very sensitive; she has inherited her father's brains and her mother's fears. She is afraid of her father, but she loves Julia Lovegrove—clings to her, in fact, as the only haven in her frightened little life.

"The servants seem to like Miss Lovegrove too. At any rate, they trust and respect her. She is far more than a governess. She is the unofficial mistress of the household. Even the pathetic madwoman trusts Miss Lovegrove and will take food from her hands, but not from those of her husband or the cook or any of the other servants. Mr. Windlesham sleeps in the little room next to his study. Miss Lovegrove sleeps on the second floor, next to Mrs. Windlesham. A door that is always left open connects the two rooms. A light is always left burning on the table in Mrs. Windlesham's room. Miss Lovegrove's bed is so placed that from it she can see, through the door, the foot of Mrs. Windlesham's bed. This is very important."

Lucy broke off and turned to look up at her husband. A little noise that sounded suspiciously like a snore had come from him. She got up from her stool.

"We are going to eat now," she said firmly, "and I shall tell you the rest while we do so."

Peter protested. "I was not asleep. I heard everything you said. The connecting door between Mrs. Windlesham's room and Miss Lovegrove's. Miss Lovegrove can always see the foot of Mrs. Windlesham's bed."

Lucy bent over and kissed him. "You are my own dearest patient Peter, and I am a selfish creature and I do not deserve you."

At this Peter protested again. When Lucy resumed her story he was fed and rested and fully awake.

"Whether any of the servants suspect that Mr. Windlesham and Miss Lovegrove have fallen in love, we do not know," she said. "Mr. Windlesham is very busy with his work and his hobbies, Miss Lovegrove very fully occupied with her duties. These include acting from time to time as his secretary and helper—in fact, doing for him the sort of service that I am doing for you, giving the sort of help that it is usual for a wife to give her husband, though not so usual, for a governess to give her employer. They are very discreet, however, so it is possible that the servants do not know, although they may suspect. Neither do the few visitors to the house— mostly professional friends of Mr. Windlesham—know anything of this guilty passion. Miss Lovegrove talks with these intelligent gentlemen on terms of equality. They respect her too. She has, on at least one occasion, attended her employer to a meeting of a learned society. Their behaviour towards each other is always perfectly proper."

"Until the declaration in the conservatory," interrupted Peter.

"And even after that, when anyone else is present. But from then on, both are consumed with the longing to be alone together, so that they can for a short while cease this pretence. It is not easy. Mrs. Windlesham is constantly crying for Julia to comfort and reassure her. She, at least, poor lady, has not the least suspicion of what is going on. Nor has the child. A shrewd young housemaid is another matter.

When she leaves to get married, the guilty couple are relieved and do not replace her. Another young servant leaves and is not replaced. There are left resident, only the cook-housekeeper whose apartments are in the basement, a kitchen-maid and a housemaid who sleep on the top floor, above Mrs. Windlesham and Miss Lovegrove, and the nurse-maid who looks after Miss Hetty. And, of course, Miss Lovegrove herself. Mr. Windlesham's manservant comes in every day but does not sleep in the house. The most convenient time for Mr. Windlesham and Miss Lovegrove to meet is in his study late at night, when the maids have all gone to bed, the child is asleep, and the mad lady is lying drugged by opiates. She is, you see, very restless in her fears, and this is the only method of ensuring that Miss Lovegrove herself has any rest. It is she who administers the drug. Mrs. Windlesham will take it from no one else."

Lucy paused for effect. They were sitting at table over the remains of their meal.

"Is she going to give Mrs. Windlesham an overdose?" asked Peter lightly. Lucy seemed to have talked herself back into her usual state of composure. Realizing that it was doing her good, Peter had forborne to point out that much of what she had been saying was already known to him from the chapters that he had himself copied. He was so glad that she was feeling better that he was happy to indulge her in her obvious pleasure in dramatic narration. In fact she was very good at it; he had not realized quite what a talent she possessed in this respect. Why, she was talking about these characters in the book just as if they were real people!

"She is not going to give Mrs. Windlesham an overdose," said Lucy. "That is not the way that Mrs. Windlesham is going to die. It is something far more cruel and distasteful than an excessive amount of laudanum."

"Good heavens!" cried Peter, "is she going to stab the mad wife to death with one of Henry Windlesham's African spears or daggers?"

"She—or rather Miss Lovegrove," said Lucy with some

severity, "does not stab Mrs. Windlesham or in fact cause her death in any other way. Not directly, that is. Not if she is to be believed. It is Mr. Windlesham himself who most ingeniously exploits the poor lady's dreadful weakness to bring about her death."

"Whatever do you mean?" asked Peter. He had stopped smiling now. Not only did Lucy's face promise some rather unpleasant revelations, but he was also beginning to feel a little disturbed by her way of talking about the people in the story.

"If she is to be believed," Lucy had said, for all the world as if Miss Julia Lovegrove, instead of being the creation of a lady author's imagination, were a witness in a lawsuit reported in the newspaper.

"Among Mrs. Windlesham's many terrors," said Lucy very seriously and with an expression of mingled pity and disgust, "was a great horror of savages—of cannibals. No doubt her husband's collection of African curios had something to do with this. Some of these things—the weapons and the masks in particular—can be very frightening even to the strong and rational mind. In fact none of the servants liked to go into Mr. Windlesham's study, where these objects were hanging on the walls and lying on the shelves, and the room was cleaned by his manservant, Roberts, an old naval man, who had seen far worse horrors of every kind during his years at sea and who was in any case a very stolid, unemotional and uncommunicative sort of individual. The child, of course, never entered the room. But Miss Lovegrove herself was a frequent visitor, and the learned friends who came to see Mr. Windlesham occasionally were also admitted to the sanctuary.

"Miss Lovegrove grew used to the hideous masks and weapons. So she says, at any rate, but even she admits that there was one particularly repulsive object—a big head-dress with coils of hair sticking out like hissing snakes and a weird, distorted, black face underneath with a gash of a mouth showing fang-like teeth. It hung on the wall just behind Mr. Windlesham's desk—perhaps he liked to show the contrast of his own distinguished handsome face with this grimacing horror as he sat there—and Miss Lovegrove states that it always gave her a slight shock when she entered the room."

Miss Lovegrove states, thought Peter. The witness in court again. But he remained silent; let Lucy tell her tale in her own way. He was indeed completely gripped by now. Lucy had as eager a listener as her dramatic instincts could demand.

"Then one November night," she went on, "when spirits are low and even stout hearts quail at the prospect of the long cold winter to come, matters came to a crisis. Poor Mrs. Windlesham was at her very worst during the month of November. It was the month when Hetty had been born, the month of the beginning of her madness. The servants were all in bed—the two girls in the attics, the cook in the basement, and the nursemaid with her little charge. Roberts had long since left the house to go to his own quarters a few streets away. The guilty lovers exchanged their passionate thoughts and still more passionate embraces, quietly, secretly in the dark and silent house. At last Julia murmured: "I must go—Laura will be wanting me, she is very restless tonight." But Henry clung to her as a drowning man clings to a lifebelt. I ought perhaps to have mentioned that although he was to all outward appearances a very strong-minded and independent and indeed rather formidable character, he presented a very different face to Julia. She saw him as bitterly unhappy behind the harshness, craving for the comfort and tenderness and affection that his unfortunate wife was no longer able to supply."

Lucy paused for a moment before saying: "I mention this in extenuation—if extenuation there can be—of what was to follow."

"And what was to follow?" asked Peter, with a not very successful attempt at lighthearted banter. "Murder most foul?"

"Yes," said Lucy frowning. "Most foul and probably quite unprovable. I cannot imagine that any jury would return a verdict of guilty, however deeply in all their hearts they felt that to be the truth, nor any judge pass sentence. The lawyer—if indeed he is a lawyer, which I take leave to doubt, although he certainly had a good knowledge of the law—would take care to choose a method that could never be brought home to him. Possibly he had been meditating over it for some time. Or perhaps the idea came to him only that very night. Julia herself believed the latter. She herself disclaims all pre-knowledge of his intentions. She swears she had not the slightest suspicion of what he was going to do, but I cannot quite make up my mind whether to believe her. She was certainly very shocked and horrified, yet it was a remark of her own that gave the inspiration for the murder. The mind is a most mysterious thing. It has strange ways of making its wishes known.''

Lucy paused again.

''What was the remark?'' asked Peter.

Dusk had fallen: the little sitting-room was dim and shadowy. They sat facing each other across the table, the lamp unlit, the curtains undrawn, intent only on each other. Lucy's hands crept across the cloth and found their way into Peter's. He held them tightly.

''Julia's remark,'' said Lucy softly, ''was that Laura was very restless and seemed to be suffering badly from her imaginary fears of savages and cannibals. 'She keeps clutching me and crying,' said Julia, 'and begging me to keep them away from her because they are coming to attack her. Sometimes I think she can actually see them—there in the room in front of her. It is very dreadful, to see a human being so mortally afraid of shadows.' That was what Julia said, and then she bade him good night and took her candle and ascended the stairs to the second floor. She found Mrs. Windlesham, whom she had left tolerably composed after a dose of her medicine, now very restless again. She soothed her as best she could, and gave her another dose of the opiate that the doctor had said might be given in emergency. She sat by the suffering lady until the latter appeared calmer, and then made herself ready to go to bed in the adjoining room,

quite prepared to be roused during the night to attend to the
invalid. In fact, the agitation of her own mind was such that
in any case sleep would have been wooed in vain. She admits
to wondering how much of the sleeping draught would be
required to ensure that Laura Windlesham would fall asleep
for ever. She admits to thinking that the death of the sick wife
would be a merciful release to everybody, including the wife
herself, whose life was nothing but painful, useless, burden-
some. And had Julia taken it into her hands to accomplish
this release, it would perhaps have been brought about more
mercifully. But it seems that Julia is not a murderer, much
though she might have longed for another woman to die, and
the release was brought about very far from mercifully."

Lucy clutched at Peter's hands, which had slightly
slackened their grip.

"Some time at dead of night," she went on, "Julia was
aroused from her half-waking, half-dreaming condition,
by a slight sound of movement from the adjoining room.
She propped herself up on one elbow and lay listening
intently, not wishing to arouse the sick lady if this were
but a false alarm and her own services not required. The
foot of Mrs. Windlesham's bed, clearly outlined by the
light that was never extinguished in that room, was visible
to Julia from where she lay. She looked and listened, hearing no further sound of movement, and was just about to
relax once more into her own uneasy dozing, when she suddenly saw, approaching the foot of Mrs. Windlesham's bed
and consequently facing its occupant, a figure the like of
which the most horrible nightmare would be hard put to it to
equal. It was wrapped in a long black cloak, round whose
hem a design of twisting snakes and other deadly creatures
was embroidered, and above this sinister garment there was
no head—or rather nothing that we would normally regard
as a human head. Instead there was a hideous, dark, grinning
face, with snake-like locks extending either side, and whitish
fangs visible in the gash of the mouth. As she watched, herself momentarily horror-stricken, gripping her bedclothes,

too paralysed to move or cry out, the figure raised one arm from under the black cloak and pointed at the occupant of the bed a deadly-looking spear.''

"Good God!" whispered Peter.

"Yes," said Lucy. "That was how it was done. Julia did not realize at the time what was happening. She was a strong-minded woman, not easily frightened, but this horrific apparition, in the half-light and shadows, at dead of night, when nerves are at their feeblest and both physical and mental resistance is low, for a few moments came not far from sending her temporarily out of her own mind. Imagine what it did to the mind and nerves of that poor, stricken crazy creature, whose life at the best of times had become a trembling mass of fears, and whose very worst fear was just such an apparition as this midnight visitor presented. Just imagine.''

"I can imagine," murmured Peter, with a face crumpled up in distaste. "I can imagine only too well. She would literally die of fright. Who would think that such a charming young lady author would invent such a horrible story as that!"

"If she did invent it," began Lucy, and then caught herself up. "Well, there is not very much more to tell," she went on after a moment's pause. "Julia heard a thin, low wail, like that of a lost soul in hell, and then a little choking gasp, a death rattle. She closed her eyes, took a deep breath, and gathered all her courage before getting out of bed. When she opened her eyes again the apparition was gone. She crept into the adjoining room and found, as she had expected, Laura Windlesham lying dead against the pillow. The white, stiffening fingers were gripping the sheets, the eyes and the mouth were wide open. There was an expression of such extreme horror upon the dead face that Julia prayed she would never have to see such a look upon any human face again.''

"And then?" prompted Peter.

Lucy, who had been gripping his hands more tightly during the last part of this recital, relaxed her grip now, and said in quite a casual voice: "Oh, the doctor ascribed the death to heart failure, of course. Mrs. Windlesham must have had a shock. He was not particularly surprised. He had been expecting something of the sort to happen one day, in view of her very weakened physical condition and the even weaker state of her mind, that saw terrors where there were none. What had actually caused her to die of fright would probably remain for ever a mystery. It might have been some trivial little incident. It would not take much to upset her tremulous balance completely. Look how she had behaved about the trees outside the window when she had lived in the front room facing the Square gardens. Perhaps the housemaid had made an unexpected sound in the room above. Who could tell what strange fantasies were in the sick woman's mind? The heart had simply ceased to beat. It was in many respects a blessed release. There had never been the slightest chance of her recovery from the dreadful sickness that had overtaken her so many years ago."

"And how does the story end?" asked Peter. "Does Julia tell Henry that she saw him dressed up like a savage to frighten his wife to death?"

"She does not tell him. She pretends to know nothing. He claims her for his own but she tells him that they must be very cautious. It would not look well to announce their engagement too soon after his wife's death. She holds him at bay, without letting him suspect that she has guessed anything, while she plans her own escape from the house and from him. A former admirer of hers, whom we have heard nothing of until this moment, suddenly appears after having been for years in India, and renews his addresses. Julia agrees to marry him, and runs away from Mr. Windlesham's house one day when he is away on business, leaving him a note telling him she is getting married to somebody else, but leaving no address for him to trace her. And there it ends. I have no belief at all in this admirer and in this elopement. If Julia is capable at all of deeply and sincerely loving any man—which I am inclined to doubt—then that man is Henry, whatever he may or may not have done. And there is no doubt whatsoever that he loves her. She would certainly not leave him for another man, and he would certainly never let her go. I simply do not believe the ending.''

''Neither does Mr. Meredith, it seems,'' said Peter, ''for he asked me to write to the author to say he wanted her to revise the last few chapters, and suggested that she should come and discuss the manuscript with him the week after next, on the Wednesday. It is to be Wednesday this time, instead of Thursday as usual, because of other engagements.''

Lucy was looking very thoughtful. ''Has the author replied?'' she asked.

''Not yet, but I am sure she will. Mr. Meredith told me to write in praise of her book. It was a fine achievement, he said, so skillfully to depict a human soul relentlessly caught up in a struggle between passion and conscience. The writing betrayed an extraordinary understanding of how an intelligent woman of strong feeling would react to such a situation. He was looking forward very much to meeting the author. We had to write Poste Restante, because she has given us no address, so it may be a day or two before we receive her reply. We invited her to 'come and meet the gentleman who has read your manuscript'—we always have to say that, you know, because no one is supposed to know who our reader is. That would not do at all.''

Lucy was drawing the curtains and lighting the lamp while Peter was speaking. When he had finished she sat down again and said in a very troubled voice: ''I am myself in some dilemma of conscience, but since I have my own dearest husband to advise me, I am going to place the burden of decision on to him.''

— 6 —

A Respectable Young Housewife Must Not
Play Detective

"You have several times reminded me," went on Lucy, "that the events I have been relating are only a story, the creation of a writer's imagination. This may be so, but I do not believe it is. I think it is very possible that most of the events recorded in this manuscript—perhaps all of them except those at the conclusion—are no invention but have actually taken place."

"But does that not," said her husband, "prove what a very fine work it is? A good writer has great power to create an illusion of reality."

Lucy made no immediate response to this, and Peter continued to press the point for several moments more. He had been more disturbed by his wife's narration than he liked to admit, and he was very much afraid that something even more worrying was to come. Lucy had that look in her eye. Peter Bond was a thoughtful and intelligent young man, very happy to be working on the fringes of the great world of literature and taking every opportunity it offered to make up for his own lack of education. Lucy knew this, and helped him tactfully in many ways, but even to her Peter had never declared his own deep secret yearning to be a writer himself. Sometimes he

thought he would pluck up courage to show some of his
poems to Mr. Meredith, who was Peter's god. In spite of
all those sarcastic comments in the manuscript register,
the great man was never personally unkind to those weaker
than himself. A poor young clerk in the office would receive more gentle handling than a friend or colleague of
equal status. It was all very well to write in secret for a
while, and there was even a strange sort of satisfaction in
overcoming the difficulty of finding an opportunity to do
the actual penning of the words; but there was bound to
come a time when you longed to show your precious trea-
sures to another human eye and to have them praised by
another human judgement. If only one could be sure that
it would be praise. That was the trouble. To have one's
work laughed at would be far worse than never showing it
at all.

Such were the thoughts that were going through Peter's
mind as he tried to convince Lucy that she had been carried away by the excellence of the story she had just read
into believing it to be true. She listened to him and agreed
with him about the powers of a good storyteller, and then
she undid all the effect of his persuasiveness by her next
remark.

"I have more solid reasons for suspecting that these
events have actually taken place. I know of a household
very like the one described in the novel."

Peter's astonished reaction was very gratifying to his
wife's dramatic instinct.

"I don't think I ever told you," she went on, "of an
experience I had a few years ago when Mr. and Mrs. Marshall were about to go abroad and I was obliged to seek
another post. There was an advertisement for a governess
to one young girl—a child of five or six—in the house of
a gentleman described as an official in the employment of
Her Majesty's Government. The duties were not onerous;
the situation of the house was very convenient, in a part
of London that I had grown to know and like. Mr. and

Mrs. Marshall, who were like father and mother to me, thought I should apply. I was not too eager to have such a very young charge—for what could I teach of music to a child aged five?—but I felt I ought to follow their advice. The house was in Russell Square, Bloomsbury.''

"Not in Kensington, as in the manuscript," put in Peter.

"And the gentleman," continued Lucy, as if he had not spoken, "was of high standing in Government. In the India Office, I believe. What I cannot remember, although no doubt if I went to some trouble I could find out, was his name. Certainly it was not Henry Windlesham. That I do know.''

"And the wife? And child?"

"The wife was an invalid and kept in her room. I remember him telling me that. The child's name I do remember, oddly enough. It was Betty. The author has not troubled to alter the truth very much there, you see—only by one letter.''

"But," protested Peter, "there must be many professional and business gentlemen living in London who have invalid wives and a child to care for. It is not such a very unusual situation for a man to be in, and they would all of them be seeking the services of a nursery governess.''

"That is true, but there is one factor that can surely apply to very few of them, and that is the collection of African masks and weapons and other curios. The gentleman to whom I applied interviewed me in his study. It was at the back of the house on the ground floor, and a small conservatory led out from it. There was a big desk and many books, and hanging on the walls was just such a collection of objects as Miss Lovegrove describes. It struck me as odd at the time that anybody should choose such ornaments for his room, for they were none of them beautiful and some were truly hideous, but the gentleman mentioned that they were of great interest to him. He told me something about his travels, I do remember that, and he

talked for a while about the education of females, on which
he held strong views. He was a handsome man, about
forty I should think. Rather stern-looking, but perfectly
courteous in his speech and his manner.''

''Did you see the wife or the child?''

''No, but I believe the child would have been brought
to me had I showed greater interest in the post. But I had
gone with some reluctance in the first place, and I decided
almost immediately that I did not wish to live and work
in that house. It was in some way very disagreeable to me.
There was something wrong, something very unhappy
there. Yes, I know, dear Peter. You may well smile, knowing that I consider myself to be a very rational creature,
not subject to whims and fancies of this nature, but in this
case I sensed an atmosphere that I did not like. Perhaps
the masks and spears had something to do with it. Perhaps
it was the cold manner in which the gentleman referred to
his wife. Perhaps I suspected that as governess I would be
obliged to come into close daily contact with him and
might even be subjected to unwelcome attentions. Or perhaps, since he really was very handsome, I was afraid that
I myself might be in danger of falling in love. I do not
know what was my reason. I only know that I felt almost
at once that this place was not for me.''

''But why did you not tell me about this before?'' asked
Peter.

''The occasion never arose. It has never occurred to me
to mention it until this moment. After all, my love, it is
not possible for me to tell you about every single thing
that has ever happened to me throughout my life, any more
than you can tell me of everything that has ever happened
to you. As you know, I have had a varied and eventful
life, and I have frequently been interviewed for situations
that I was not offered or did not choose to take. Believe
me, dear, I was not being unduly secretive in never mentioning this matter to you before.''

Peter, who sometimes had a slight tendency to think

enviously of Lucy's eventful life in comparison with his own much narrower experience, suddenly remembered that he himself was being exceedingly secretive about something that mattered a great deal to him—his own literary ambitions—and he hastened to reassure her that he had not intended any reproach. He even admitted that it was very odd indeed that the gentleman who had interviewed her should so closely resemble the hero of *A Most Mysterious Death*.

"Presumably Miss Faith Freeman alias Miss Julia Lovegrove alias whatever her real name is, required employment more urgently than I did at that time," said Lucy. "Or perhaps she was made of tougher metal than I, and did not have those doubts and misgivings that led me to withdraw my application for the post."

"Suppose you had taken it!" cried Peter. "You would never have gone to work for those friends of the Chapmans and we would never have met."

"And instead of sitting here cosily with my darling, and looking forward eagerly to the arrival of our little darling, I might have been in the position of the unfortunate Faith or Julia or whatever her name really is—having a man commit murder for my sake, and feeling so terribly guilty about it that I confided the whole story to paper. Though I do not think," added Lucy, after a moment's thought, "that I should have been so exceedingly rash and indiscreet as to offer the manuscript for publication to a firm of publishers."

"I am not so sure," said Peter, rather to Lucy's surprise. "I think you might have been sorely tempted to do so, when you realized how well you had told the story, and what an exceedingly fascinating and arresting account it was. Mr. Meredith thinks very highly indeed of the book. It is not often that an unknown author wins his good opinion in this manner."

"It is very well written, it is very striking, it is indeed a most wonderful book," admitted Lucy. "I think perhaps you are right, dear. I think perhaps it is hardly in human nature to write such a book and then put it away unread and unseen by any other human eye, whatever risk one was taking in letting it be seen, quite apart from the fact that one would, in a way, feel that one was expiating one's own feeling of guilt. And she has, of course, gone to some pains to disguise the house and its owner.''

"If you are right in your assumption that it is the same house," pointed out Peter.

"I am sure I am. And there is another thing." Lucy paused: Peter looked at her unhappily. "I notice that the author seemed uncertain as to the name of the parlour-maid at one point," continued Lucy. "She calls her first one name and then another. You will notice if you copy that part. I was sorely tempted to correct the mistake—you know I cannot abide inconsistencies of that kind—but of course I know I must make no mark on the manuscript.''

Peter, who had for a moment looked quite appalled, relaxed again.

"In any case it is a trivial error," went on Lucy, "and I would probably not have troubled to mention it had not a more serious change of name occurred several times later on, when Mrs. Windlesham is referred to not as 'Laura' but as 'Louisa'. Now why should this be? You will say there is a perfectly innocent explanation, but for my part I should be extremely interested to know whether the wife of the gentleman who interviewed me was called Louisa. I wonder whether there is any way in which I could find out.''

"Lucy!" This time Peter's alarm showed in his voice. "You are not really going to make any such attempt?''

"I don't quite see how I can," said Lucy regretfully. "I could probably identify the house—it was next door to one that was once inhabited by Samuel Romilly, the great philanthropist, but I simply cannot remember the gentleman's name, and I can hardly ring the bell and ask if the owner once had a wife named Louisa.''

''I should hope not indeed!'' cried Peter.

''Of course there are private detectives who are expert at this sort of thing,'' went on Lucy, following her own train of thought regardless of Peter's interruption, ''but they cost money. I suppose I might hang about outside the house and try to get into conversation with one of the servants.''

Peter stared at her. ''You cannot be serious,'' he said at last.

Lucy came out of her thoughts, saw his expression, and smiled. ''Poor Peter,'' she said affectionately. ''Are you regretting that you married me? No, dear, you are quite right. I am only half serious. There are a lot of things that I should like to do but that I realize I ought not to.''

Once again Peter's face showed his relief. He would have been hard put to it to explain exactly why the notion of Lucy carrying out detective work on her own in one of the great squares of Bloomsbury should have been so utterly repulsive to him, for his distaste was compounded of many different elements. There was envy of her past life, resentment and even a little fear of her independence and strong will, and an overall feeling—for Peter took a conventional view of the place of women—that it was unsuitable and somehow indecent for a wife who should be thinking only of her coming motherhood to be exercising her wits in this matter that was really his own concern, not hers, and that would never have come to her notice at all if he had not told her about it.

But among the more selfish and less worthy considerations, there was also a strong concern for Lucy's own safety and wellbeing. If she was right in her supposition about the manuscript—and Peter had to admit that she had made out a good case—then it could lead her not only into unpleasantness, but perhaps even into positive danger, if she were to go making enquiries. He said this aloud. Lucy could hardly blame him for not wanting her to run into serious trouble.

"Yes, dear, I know," she replied. "It would be unwise if I were to meddle in this case and I promise you I will do nothing, provided you take some action about it yourself, for I really do think that something ought to be done."

"But what action can I take?" asked Peter, stalling for time. He had a strong suspicion of what was coming; he might have known that all Lucy's talk of carrying out detective work was only a prelude to manoeuvring her husband into doing something that he would rather not do. "Do you want me to go and talk to housemaids in Russell Square?"

"No indeed," cried Lucy, laughing. "I certainly do not. One of them might be prettier than me! If it comes to investigating, we will do it together. But it is not really our business. It is up to the gentlemen who are responsible for the running of your firm."

"And you think I ought to tell them about this notion of yours?"

"Well, dear, it is of course for you to decide," said Lucy primly. "I have no knowledge of publishing or of the gentlemen in question."

"I don't know what to do." Peter ran his fingers through his hair. "I was not supposed to tell anybody else about the manuscript in the first place."

"But they would notice the different handwriting. You would have to admit that I had helped you in any case."

"Our writings are not dissimilar. It is not very likely that anybody will look closely at the copy unless the original should become lost or damaged."

Lucy made no comment. She was determined both that Peter should decide this matter for himself and that he should make the right decision. She had known when she married him that he had a tendency to hesitate and to shirk from taking firm action; she was confident of possessing determination enough for two, but nevertheless he ought not to grow to depend upon her all the time. He must at any rate give the appearance of making up his own mind.

"In any case," said Peter presently, "we have not even finished the copying yet. There will be plenty of time to decide whether or not to mention your experience when I hand over the copy and the original manuscript."

Lucy was sewing. She broke off a thread with a sharp snap, but still said nothing.

Peter spread out his writing materials and remarked that there would just be time to do a little more of the copying tonight.

"Well, dear," Lucy greeted him some evenings later. "Was Mr. Chapman pleased to have the copy of *A Most Mysterious Death*?"

"Oh yes. He was surprised to have it so quickly. I am to have the extra money next week." Peter's manner was studiedly casual and he hurried on to talk of something else.

He has not told them, said Lucy to herself; I was afraid he would not, once he began to find an excuse to delay.

"Yes, dear," she said aloud in response to her husband's remarks. "Your mother came this afternoon and brought these caps for the baby. Aren't they pretty?"

She chatted brightly about their domestic affairs, but did not fail to notice how relieved Peter looked when no further word was said about the manuscript of *A Most Mysterious Death*. I will wait and see, she said to herself, until after the author has made her visit to the offices of Chapman and Hall. Peter will be bound to tell me all he knows of the result of that interview, and if it seems as if they are going to publish the book, then I shall have to do something about it myself if he still refuses to act.

After all, Peter was thinking as he continued to talk about his mother's visit and the baby's clothes, Lucy does not understand what it is like in the office. She has no idea what a tyrant old Chapman is. I cannot go to him and say: Look here, you must not publish this book, it would be libellous, my wife says that they are real people. It would be quite out of place; he would only shout at me and I might even lose my job. Lucy might get away with it herself, of course. A woman often does get away with things when a poor fellow hasn't a chance. But there it is, that is the unfairness of it all. And she will never understand. She may have had to earn her own living, but she has always worked with people who treated her like a daughter. She has no conception of what business life is like.

Thus Peter excused himself to himself. But he was not at all happy about it. Quite apart from the unpleasant awareness that underneath all her surface chatter, Lucy was silently disappointed in him, his own conscience was telling him that murder was something about which one ought not to keep silent. A man who had killed once might well kill again. Ought not this beautiful young woman, whom Tom the office boy was still dreaming about, to be protected from the consequences of her own rashness?

Oh, it is none of my business, he exclaimed to himself impatiently several times: I cannot tell my superiors how they ought to run the firm. You ought to tell them, a little voice replied; it is your duty. Conscience, aided by the misery of feeling disapproved of by Lucy, won a tiny victory in the end. I will wait until Wednesday, Peter decided, and will find some opportunity to speak to Mr. Meredith alone after he has interviewed the lady. If we are going to publish the book I will tell him what Lucy has told me; if not, then I will forget the whole thing.

7

Can You Swear That This Murder Has Not Taken Place?

Just under three weeks after the lady in black had first visited the offices of Messrs. Chapman and Hall, Tom Stiles, feeling now sufficiently at ease at his post to whistle when Mr. Goodbody was out of earshot, repeated over and over to himself: this afternoon I shall see her, I shall see her today. He might have said it aloud without causing much surprise, for all the clerks in the office, not only his special friend Peter Bond, were very well aware of the boy's romantic attachment.

The lady in black had, in fact, already become something of a legend at Chapman and Hall in other minds as well as that of the office boy. The clerks were not so busy that they did not find time to gossip now and then, and gossip had it that Mr. Meredith was exceedingly impressed by the lady's novel but that Mr. Chapman and the other directors were very worried about it for some reason or other. What this reason was, nobody knew; nor did anybody except Peter know what the book was about. Peter had been told to keep quiet about the making of the copy, and this he had done. The copy was now safely resting in a drawer at Mr. Chapman's home at Banstead in Surrey. The original manuscript was also in Surrey, in

the chalet above Flint Cottage, where Mr. Meredith had
taken it after the copy had been made, in order to refresh
his memory on one or two points before discussing its
revision with the author.

While Tom was whistling away in happy anticipation of
once again seeing the charming lady in black and in sheer
joy of life this fine sunny morning, Mr. Meredith, in a
very bad temper, was putting the manuscript in a case
together with other papers in preparation for the day's
business in London. He was short of sleep, having been
writing for half the night again, and the brilliant sky and
the sparkling hillside were calling to him to refresh both
body and mind. A twenty-mile tramp over those green
hills and through the budding beechwoods would be just
the thing to put him into a fit condition to write again. To
walk all day, then come back in the cool of the evening,
have a meal and a chat with Marie, then back to the chalet
to proceed steadily with the history of *Diana of the Crossways*—that was the sort of programme that he would have
chosen for himself.

Instead of this he was going to get into a dirty, stuffy
train, come out into even dirtier and more stifling streets,
listen to the worries of old Fred and two of the other directors, and sit in a small and sunless room at the back of
the building, telling a young woman that she was going to
have to alter her story and incidentally try to get her to
confess whether or not the story was a true one. It was no
longer of any interest to him that she had reminded him,
at the first fleeting glance, of his own Diana. She could
have been the goddess herself, and it would have been just
the same. He wanted a long country walk and then to get
on with his own writing: he did not want to struggle up
to London only to have to talk about other people's.

"I'm sick to death of it," he said angrily to Marie.

She kissed him but made no reply. She had heard this
before. There was no point in saying anything. George
would go on driving himself too hard and no one and

nothing on earth would stop him. He lived on his nerves—perhaps this was the only way he could live, and the wonder was that they seemed to provide him with such a nourishing diet. All that she could do was just be there when needed. She turned her mind to the tasks of the day and looked forward to the pleasure of a couple of hours at the piano when her duties were completed.

"Here she comes!" hissed Tom to Peter Bond a few hours later. He had escaped from Mr. Goodbody's surveillance for long enough to go to the door and see the lady in black walking slowly along Henrietta Street. It was part of his duties to attend to visitors. He stood by his stool pretending to be very absorbed in the address on a package that he was to deliver by hand later that afternoon, but all the time his ears were alert for her footsteps. Would she recognize him? Would she smile at him when she spoke, as if they were old friends? Tom lived through a few terrible moments when he feared that she would not remember. And then at last all the waiting was over. She was standing just inside the front office as she had stood before, veiled and dressed in black, greeting him very kindly, trusting that he was enjoying his work, and hoping she was not late for her appointment with the gentleman who had read her manuscript.

"Indeed you're not, ma'am," said Tom. "You are just right. Mr.—er, I mean our reader—has just been down to tell me I was to bring you up when you arrived and not waste time running up and down announcing you and all that sort of silly caper."

The lady in black smiled. "I rather like the sound of Mr. er—your reader," she said. "Do you think he will like me?"

"Oh yes! I am sure he will," cried the delighted Tom. "Will you come this way, please, ma'am? Excuse me if I lead the way. The stairs are rather dark. If you would be so kind as to follow me."

So eager was Tom both to feast his eyes on his heroine

and to ensure that she did not take a false step, that he himself negotiated the steep staircase sideways, in awkward crablike fashion. And then it all came to an end even more quickly than he had anticipated. He had not even the glory of throwing open the door of the inner office for her and bowing her in. Mr. Meredith himself emerged from Mr. Chapman's room just as Tom and the visitor reached the top of the stairs, said abruptly, "Miss Faith Freeman? Will you come this way, madam?" and there was nothing left for Tom but to return to his dull work of addressing circulars in the chivvying presence of Mr. James Goodbody.

The lady in black seated herself on a straight-backed, leather-covered chair, folded her hands lightly together, rested them on the edge of the desk, and looked with great composure at the grey-haired gentleman sitting opposite her. If she was nervous, there was not the least hint of it in her bearing. On the contrary, there was a little complacent smile on the lips just visible beneath the lace veil, the smile of one who, unknown to his opponent, holds a trump card.

Mr. Meredith noticed the smile, but not knowing its cause, became more irritable than ever.

"You will have been informed that we think very highly of your novel, madam," he said, placing a hand on the manuscript that lay on the desk between them.

"I have indeed, and I am deeply gratified—deeply honoured would perhaps be a better word—at having won such an opinion from such a source."

She smiled again, and received a very suspicious glance from the shrewd blue eyes.

"You will also have been informed that we should like you to consider the possibility of revising certain sections of the manuscript before we make an offer for its publication."

"Yes, sir. That was stated in the letter. Which are the sections that do not meet with your approval?"

"Let us deal with the least important first. I have marked a few passages which will need some modification in order not to offend the sensibilities of Mrs. Grundy. Unfortunately she is still active, even in this year of grace. The great British public delights to wallow in a haze of sentimentality. Scenes of genuine passion it will not stomach."

The lady in black coloured faintly behind her veil.

"You think I have been too outspoken, sir?" she said falteringly.

"*I* do not think so," was the vigorous reply. "Please do not attribute such sentiments to *me*. It is not to my taste to give such advice. I abhor hypocrisy and cant with all my heart. It is my duty to warn you of the likely reactions of readers and reviewers."

"I understand, sir," said the lady softly, and with a glance of sympathy.

Mr. Meredith had indeed spoken with great bitterness, inwardly wincing. It was not doing his temper any good at all to be thus forcibly reminded of how some of his own greatest work had been very nearly strangled in infancy, banned by the circulating libraries, viciously attacked by critics as indecent and obscene, not fit to be perused by the members of any respectable household. True, events had changed for the better for him since then, but these early wounds had cut very deep and left scars that never ceased to ache.

"That is agreed, then," he said crisply, turning over the pages of the manuscript as he spoke. "You will have no difficulty, with your talents, in revising these marked passages. We come now to a major problem, and that is the ending. The long lost admirer from overseas. The elopement. That is not convincing. That is simply not true."

Again she flushed faintly. "I would rather not alter the ending," she said. "I am sorry you do not like it."

"Nobody will like it, except those whose minds do not rise above a penny novelette, and your novel is not for

them. It could—it should—take its place among the greatest were the last few chapters equal to the rest of the
book.''

"I am flattered to hear you say so," replied the visitor,
turning her head aside.

Mr. Meredith waved a hand impatiently. "This is no
flattery. This is the truth. Are you or are you not willing
to re-write the end?''

The lady in black made no reply.

"It will not do, believe me. It is flat, tagged-on, quite
insincere. After the power and the truth of the book it is
a most awkward and sentimental little tailpiece of invention.''

"But the whole book is invention!" cried the lady with
some spirit.

"Is it, madam? Can you swear that to me?''

Again she sat silent.

"Can you swear that these characters are not living,
breathing people—those of them who are still alive, that
is? Living people who have gone through just such experiences as are described therein?'' Mr. Meredith again laid
his hand on the manuscript. "Can you swear it?''

The visitor gripped her hands together to hide their
trembling as she replied in an agitated voice.

"Surely no author can ever swear that he has in no way
drawn upon a living person—we can write only from our
own experiences and our own observation—we have no
other source. We must draw from life, surely we must!''

"We must and should draw from life, but we must do
it with a certain degree of caution.''

"And that I have done," broke in the lady.

"Particularly," continued Mr. Meredith, "when we are
writing of events that present our characters in an unfa-
vourable light. Should we depict them as committing
crimes, the caution must be that much the stronger—in
fact it is most inadvisable to portray them as breaking the
law at all when we are drawing so plainly from life. I can

think of no degree of caution, no method of disguise, that would be adequate for our security if the crime be murder."

"Oh!" The lady gave a little gasp and raised her hands to her face.

"However," said Mr. Meredith blandly, "you are assuring me that the account of the murder contained in your novel is pure invention, every bit of it, so any warning is clearly unnecessary." He paused, turning over pages in a casual manner before continuing in very matter-of-fact tones: "We have a form of legal contract, of course, setting out the financial and other arrangements and obliging the author to guarantee to the publisher that the manuscript contains no libellous matter. You would, no doubt, be willing to put your signature to such a guarantee?"

A sound came from the lady in black that was quite clearly distinguishable as a moan.

"You would not?" Mr. Meredith raised his eyebrows as if in surprise. "My dear young lady, we cannot possibly consider publication except under such warrant from the author. This is a business firm that has to make its profit in order to survive. It is not in a position to cast away thousands of pounds on libel actions."

"Oh, my God!" The lady in black covered her face with her hands. "I had not thought of that. Whatever shall I do?"

This time it was Mr. Meredith's turn to remain unhelpfully silent.

"I have been so perplexed and distressed about it all," continued the lady, "that sometimes I have felt there was no way out of my difficulty save death."

She sounded distressed enough now, but there was something a trifle stagy about her manner, as if she was calculating the effect of her words on her hearer. She was no longer speaking with the spontaneity with which her earlier cry of alarm had broken from her.

"I sometimes feel that there is no solution save in death," she murmured.

"All living creatures feel that from time to time," said Mr. Meredith presently, forced by the silence into making some sort of response. "Death is that friend without whom life would be insupportable."

"You are harsh, sir," she said.

"I am truthful, madam. It might save us all a considerable amount of trouble if you would be the same."

The lady in black took a small handkerchief from the black silk bag that she carried and dabbed at her eyes under the veil before she spoke again.

"I am so alone," she said. "If only I had somebody to help and advise me. Please, please help me, Mr. Meredith!"

Her voice was low and sweet and pleading: it was designed to melt a stone.

"The devil!" exclaimed Mr. Meredith, giving a violent start. "How do you come to know my name?"

— 8 —

A Clever Gentleman Is Almost Outwitted

"Please do not be angry with me," said the lady in black. "I recognized you as soon as I came in. It was quite by chance, I do assure you. I saw you when I first came here to deliver the manuscript a few weeks ago. I did not know you then, but I could not help wondering who you were—you did not look to me quite the sort of person who—"

She broke off in some confusion.

"Perhaps you will be so kind as to remind me," said Mr. Meredith icily, "of the occasion on which I had the honour of making your acquaintance. I confess that for the moment it escapes me."

"It was at a meeting of the Shelley Society last week, at the dramatic reading of a little-known work of the poet's. We were not introduced, sir. I am not presuming to claim acquaintance with you. I was a very humble visitor at the back of the room. You were among the ranks of the famous in front. It was a young man who seemed to be very interested in the drama, a Mr. Shaw, who pointed you out to me, together with other celebrities. You were seated near to Mr. Robert Browning and Mr. Russell Lowell and Mr. Andrew Lang."

"Madam," he interrupted, "you need bring no further evidence of my presence on that occasion. I do not deny

75

it. I am not trying to claim an alibi. In the matter of identity, however, you have the advantage of me.''

''I cannot tell you my real name, Mr. Meredith. Indeed I dare not. Please do not bully me.''

''Bully!'' echoed Mr. Meredith in disgust. ''I am not bullying you. I am not a police officer. It is your own conscience that makes enquiries painful. I am not asking you your name. I am only requesting that you will respect mine. The world of literature is a small one—a jealous and gossiping world. It is surely not necessary to point out to you how very desirable it is, on all counts, that a man whose task it is to decide upon the fate of manuscripts and authors should remain, as far as possible, anonymous.''

''I shall respect your wishes, Mr. Meredith. As an ardent admirer of your works, I count it a great privilege to talk with you.''

''Madam, I am not to be flattered.''

''No, sir, but champion of women that you are, you are to be appealed to by a woman who is desperately in need of intelligent advice and cool judgement.''

''As a literary adviser I have given you my opinion of your work.''

''You have indeed, sir, and it is an opinion far beyond my dreams. It is that that has placed me in a cruel dilemma. Had you thought ill of my work I should not be in this difficulty.''

''I cannot think ill of your work in order to make life easy for you.''

''But of my character? You must surely think ill of that? You would condemn me?''

These questions were asked eagerly, breathlessly, the dark eyes glistening behind the veil, the full lips slightly parted.

''It is not part of my duties,'' said Mr. Meredith coldly, ''to think anything about your character at all.''

''But as a man—as a writer—as a great writer, you must

surely be interested in this question of conscience. The pressing burden of a secret—the need to ease the mind's conflict by finding words to describe it—"

"If you have a confession to make, madam, you should seek a priest!"

"I want no priest! I want advice!" cried the lady passionately. "You said yourself just now that writers must draw from life. Supposing that you, as a writer, were to draw a character from someone very dear to you—someone who had perhaps committed some grievous sin—"

She broke off. Mr. Meredith had gone very pale. His lips twitched and it was a moment or two before he could control them enough to speak.

"You are presumptuous, madam," he said at last. "I have never, to my knowledge, been an accessory to murder, nor, so far as I am aware, have I ever been responsible for a fellow creature's death. In that respect, at least, my conscience is clear."

"I beg your forgiveness, sir," said the lady, rather taken aback by the violence of the response to what she had regarded as a purely hypothetical suggestion, "if I have unwittingly distressed you. I intended no offence."

Mr. Meredith recovered himself. He really must be very tired indeed, he decided, to be so easily provoked into biting inwardly upon unhealed wounds, by a woman who was not in the least like his first wife, and who had in fact nothing personally to do with him at all.

"We were speaking of literary advice," he said coolly. "My advice to you, if you seek a career in literature, is to put aside this manuscript and to write another novel on a completely different theme, drawing on other people's lives and characters only to an extent that will cause no offence and put nobody at risk."

"I do not know whether I could do that," she said doubtfully. "I do not know whether I could write on any other theme with the urgency and the emotion that I have put into this novel."

"Then you are no writer, madam."

"But you have just said that I am!"

"I have said that this book is a fine one. That is all."

"And critics will praise it? And people will admire my gifts?"

She was almost childishly eager now.

"I have no doubt of it. Provided the ending is revised."

She made no comment.

"You are ambitious," he said. "You are anxious for praise."

"Yes!" It was spoken with surprising force. "Is that a crime? A crime in a woman to have brains and ambition? For shame, Mr. Meredith. You who have written 'More brain, oh Lord, more brain,' you who have pleaded so eloquently in your writings for women to have the right to feel and think and speak! You of all men cannot think so."

"No, I do not think so," he said, frowning. "It is no crime in a woman to be ambitious, to seek to be herself. It is no crime in anyone to long for recognition. Provided they are prepared to pay the price."

"And the price in my case is—?"

Mr. Meredith rose to his feet. "Madam, I cannot answer that question," he said in an exasperated voice. "I have made the position perfectly clear. We will reconsider your manuscript if you will alter the ending and if you will guarantee that it contains no libellous matter. The price that you might have to pay in your own life and your own feelings is known to you alone."

"And that is your last word?"

Her voice was trembling now: she sounded very close to tears.

Mr. Meredith drew a deep breath. "What else am I to say? This is not a confessional, it is not a court of justice, it is the office of a firm of publishers, and I am their reader, and I am carrying out my duties to the best of my ability. And I have many other pressing matters to attend to, so you will excuse me—"

He laid a hand on the manuscript of *A Most Mysterious Death* and pushed it towards her. She snatched it up, rose to her feet, burst into tears, dropped the manuscript on the desk again, and rushed out of the room, sobbing violently and dabbing at her face with her handkerchief.

Mr. Meredith sank back into his chair again and for one of the few times in his life sat and swore, not in the boisterous way in which Mr. Chapman was accustomed to swear at his staff, but quietly and with a much more vivid and varied command of language. When he had relieved his feelings a little, he said to himself: She is guilty of something, but in what way and to what extent, God knows. Lady Macbeth? Or something more complicated? In any case, I pity the poor foolish devil who has tied himself up with her. Though really it is difficult to see how he could have avoided it. What a woman! What an actress! And what a writer.

He stood up again, assembled the manuscript pages that had scattered when the author dropped them on the desk before her flight, and took the book into Mr. Chapman's office. Mr. Chapman was not there. Mr. Meredith cleared a place for the manuscript amongst the jumbled mess of books and documents on the desk, found a loose sheet of paper and wrote on it: "It is as I thought, Fred. I think you should do something about it quickly." He put this message on top of the manuscript and secured it by a paperweight. Then he returned to the back room, collected his own belongings, and hurried out of the building without calling out his usual cheerful goodbye to the clerks in the front office.

Peter Bond, who had for some time been sitting idle at his desk with his eyes on the entrance to the office, heard the steps on the stairs but arrived at the street door too late. Mr. Meredith was walking at a great pace in the direction of Charing Cross Station. Peter Bond stood looking disconsolately after him.

Later that afternoon, in the garden of Flint Cottage,

with the light breeze bringing white flakes of cherry blossom down on to the bright green grass, and the barking of the dachshund now distant, now near at hand, Marie Meredith heard for the first time the whole story of the manuscript of *A Most Mysterious Death*. It was very rarely that anything ruffled her placidity, but she did look a little surprised when he concluded.

"But is that possible," she said, "to be guilty and to make it publicly known in such a manner?"

"Yes, yes, it's perfectly possible," said her husband impatiently. "It is just the sort of thing I should do myself."

"My dear George!" For once she really looked quite shocked.

"I mean," he said frowning, "that an experience such as this will find its way out somehow. In a writer it will find its way out in words. She is a very good writer. She knows it and she longs for recognition. She still wants the novel published, in spite of everything."

"How can you know that?"

"She changed her mind at the last minute and left the manuscript in the office. In moments of fury or distress it is our actions that tell the truth."

Marie Meredith stared at him. Even after all these years, there were times when George was still capable of disconcerting her.

"Nevertheless I do not see," she said very firmly, "that you could possibly have done anything other than what you did."

"Neither do I," he replied, "and yet I feel at fault. I have botched it somehow. The very worst torment that a human being can suffer is the torment of guilt. She wanted to confess to me and I would not let her."

"But why on earth should you be obliged to hear her confession? There are priests for her to go to if she needs to confess. Even if she is not a Catholic they would hear her."

"Yes, yes. So I told her. But they would not understand her need to write and publish the story. She wanted to tell a writer, who would understand."

"And transfer her burden of guilt on to you who are already burdened enough in so many ways," said Marie bitterly. "Of course you did right to resist it. You do far more work for Chapman and Hall than they have any right to expect for the salary. On top of that you spend hours of your own time writing to young authors and encouraging them. You take on work for the newspapers, work for the reviews, you never refuse a request, and you sit up all night writing your own novels. You also have a wife and a home and a family. Please do not forget that."

"I am sorry, Marie," said George, in humble tones that no one else ever heard from him. "Please forgive me."

A little later he said: "You will have guessed one of the reasons why this business has particularly worried me."

"Yes. That she recognized you. That is most unfortunate."

"It is a pity you were not able to come with me that evening. You might have taken more notice of the ladies present."

"But perhaps that is not so unfortunate. You do not really want to know who she is."

"I do and I don't. It might be most embarrassing, particularly if—" He broke off.

"If?" prompted Marie.

"It is most unlikely," he replied in an agitated voice, "that she came to that meeting of the Shelley Society alone. I did not gain the impression that she was herself a member. It was a private meeting; she could only have been there as somebody's guest."

"Oh, I see." Dawning awareness showed in Marie Meredith's eyes. "And that somebody is only too likely to be—"

"—the man with whom, in spite of the patched-on ending of the novel, her whole life is inextricably involved.

That he is a man of culture is very evident from the manuscript.''

''Oh dear,'' said Marie.

Husband and wife gazed at each other in sympathetic communion of thought.

''Who amongst our acquaintance,'' asked George, ''has quite possibly disposed of his sick wife in order to marry his brilliant and fascinating mistress?''

''That settles it,'' said Marie. She got up from the garden seat and brushed the petals of cherry blossom off her dress. ''We are going to take a holiday. As soon as you are free of your most urgent commitments we shall go to Normandy. I will write today.''

George did not assent but neither did he make any protest.

9

An Unhappy Man Receives a Very Dusty Answer

Shortly before the moment when Peter Bond had stood looking unhappily along Henrietta Street at the retreating figure of Mr. Meredith, Tom Stiles, also in a state of agitation, had been hovering around the street door. Mr. Goodbody had informed him that he positively must not delay another minute before delivering that package that had been entrusted to him. It contained urgent proofs for correction by the author, who lived in the neighbourhood of Regent's Park. It was quite a distance away, and at the rate Tom was going, he would scarcely get there and back this afternoon.

"Be off with you, lad," he concluded.

Tom was obliged to pick up the package and open the door, but just before closing it behind him he listened to Mr. Goodbody telling Peter Bond that he must go and see one of the gentlemen in the Counting House about a complaint by another author concerning the non-receipt of a cheque. The Counting House was at the other end of the building. That means he will be gone some time, said Tom to himself, his ear to the crack in the door; I can hang about a little longer; Peter will not tell if he sees me. Tom's reluctance to depart was, of course, due to his desire to see the lady in black again.

Luck was on his side. A very few moments after Mr.
Goodbody had departed on his errand through the inner
door of the front office, Tom heard the sound of a door
opening on the floor above, followed by quick footsteps
on the stairs. He stepped out into the street and waited at
one side of the front door. He did not want to get in her
way; he only wanted to look at her and smile at her as she
passed. And perhaps she would smile at him. Surely she
must be happy. It was known throughout the office how
very highly Mr. Meredith thought of her book.

It was with surprise as well as with concern that he saw
the black-clad figure hurrying down the steep stairs at
breakneck speed, not looking where she was going and
obviously in great distress, with her handkerchief held to
her face. She came through the door and out into the street
without noticing Tom, rushed blindly across the road, nar-
rowly escaping being run down by a drayhorse, and disappeared down the narrow alleyway that led to the Church
of St Paul's, Covent Garden.

Tom moved with almost equal speed. Stopping only to
avoid the horse and cart, he raced across the road and
through the archway to the churchyard. There he stopped
and looked at the other exit for a moment before he realized that she was only a few feet away from him, seated
on one of the wooden benches on the broad pathway between the gravestones. Her face was buried in her hands
and her shoulders were heaving. There was, at that moment, no other person in sight in the churchyard.

Tom stood uncertainly watching her and clutching the
package he was supposed to be delivering. Surely Mr.
Meredith could not have said something unkind to her
about her book after all? It seemed the only possible explanation for her tears, but Tom found it very difficult to
believe. He had seen a lot of the workings of the office
since the day when he had naïvely supposed that authors
were always told the reader's opinion of their work, and
he had also, following his friend Peter Bond, himself be-

gun to develop something of a hero-worshipping attitude towards Mr. Meredith. But whatever else could be the matter? He had seen the lady walk upstairs, charming and dignified and composed, to discuss the publication of her novel with the reader; and he had seen her, not much more than half an hour later, rush downstairs distraught and weeping as if her heart would break. Had some bad news been brought to her in the meantime, while she was there in the office?

After a few minutes the lady in black became calmer, removed her handkerchief from her eyes, adjusted her veil, got to her feet, and walked slowly out of the churchyard. She had not noticed Tom at all; he did not think that she was noticing anything in the world about her. It had been in his mind to speak to her and ask if he could be of any help, but the thought seemed silly now, because there was nothing that he could offer to do. When she had reached the far end of the churchyard he began to walk after her, his feet seeming to move of their own accord without him telling them to. She did not look back. She seemed to be totally unaware of her surroundings, deeply sunk in her own despair, finding her way by instinct, like an animal.

He followed her along the crowded pavements of Long Acre and Drury Lane, past St. George's Church, through some little streets behind the big squares of Bloomsbury, until at last they emerged into a great square where tall houses surrounded a garden containing bushes and plane trees. Russell Square, said Tom to himself, suddenly remembering that he was supposed to be delivering a package to near Regent's Park and noting, with relief that he was after all not going so very far out of his way. The lady looked left and right and then crossed the roadway and walked on to the far side of the square, still quite unconscious of being followed. Tom, in spite of his sympathy for her, could not help but feel a little excited at the thought that he was playing detective.

He sidled along by the railings, prepared at any moment, should she turn round, to be seen hanging over them as if trying if it were possible to climb into the garden, until at last she reached her destination. At the broad, low doorstep of one of the big houses on the far side of the square she paused and opened her little purse. Then suddenly she looked up. Tom instinctively drew back a step, but she was not looking towards him. A girl dressed as a nursemaid was approaching the house from the opposite direction, holding by the hand a little girl whom even at this distance Tom saw to be walking listlessly, unhappily, with none of the lively eagerness of a child being taken for a walk. It seemed to him that the little girl came to life somewhat when she saw the lady in black, for she let go of the nursemaid's hand and ran towards her. The lady in black lifted her veil, bent down, and kissed the child. Then they all three entered the house together and Tom was left staring at a big black front door. Well, at least I know where she lives, he thought: Number twenty-two Russell Square, and then he exclaimed to himself: "Crikey! I'll never be back in time to do the post. I'll be in terrible hot water with Mr. Goodbody."

He clutched the parcel more firmly under his arm and began to run, knocking into passers-by and dashing across roadways without stopping to look whether any vehicles were approaching, and leaving in his wake a train of cursing cab-drivers, and pedestrians exclaiming "What a rude and careless boy!" I know where she lives, he was saying to himself, and it is not all that very far to walk from Camberwell, and if I can get away from Ma some evening I shall come over here and have a look at her house again.

The object of his thoughts had by this time taken off her hat, kissed the little girl again, and said: "Run along and tell Mrs. Greenaway that we are all in, Betty. We will have tea together in the nursery, shall we?"

The child ran off and the lady turned to the nursemaid and said, with the smile fading from her face: "She looks so pale and tired. Did she take no pleasure at all in going to the park?"

"I hardly know, ma'am, I mean, Miss Brown." The girl spoke uncertainly, as if not quite sure how to address the questioner. She was hardly more than a child herself, and had been only a few weeks in this her very first post. "She did say something about the animals, but I did not quite like to take her to the Zoo, not on my own."

"You decided quite right, Clara. It would have been too much exertion for her. Besides, you would have needed the money for the entrance fee. But we will go to the Zoo, that is a very good idea. We will go together, the three of us, in a cab. And spend all afternoon there. Should you like that?"

"Oh yes, ma'am." The girl's eyes lighted up. A moment later she realized that she ought to have said "Miss Brown," because Mrs. Greenaway, the cook-housekeeper, had dinned it into her that Miss Brown was really only the governess, a paid servant like themselves. Not that Mrs. Greenaway, who was a kindly soul, disliked Miss Brown—nobody could possible dislike her, she was so calm and kind and always seemed to know what was worrying you even before you said it—but Mrs. Greenaway did like people to be given their proper places, and Miss Brown was not the mistress of the house, even if Mr. Mackay did treat her with such respect.

"And more than respect, if you ask me," Mrs. Greenaway had said to Clara on her very first evening. "She could be Mrs. Lawrence Mackay tomorrow if she chose, in my opinion. Why she does not choose—well, that is something I shall never understand."

"Is the master not married, then?" Clara had timidly asked.

"He is a widower," was the reply. "His wife died about eighteen months ago, but she could have been dead long before that for all the life she led, poor lady. She never recovered after Miss Betty was born—poor sickly little thing the baby was too. Nobody thought it would live. It did, though, but it had nearly killed the mother.''

''Oh dear,'' murmured Clara sympathetically. ''How very sad.''

''She kept her room for more than seven years,'' went on the housekeeper, ''and then she died quite suddenly one night. Some little shock had brought about heart failure, the doctor said. She was very subject to such shocks. The least little sound would set her all a-trembling and when she was very bad she could not bear anybody near her—only Miss Brown. I do not know what we should have done without Miss Brown, and it is no wonder to me that Mr. Mackay, now the mourning period for his wife is over and he is free—but no matter, I was talking of Mrs. Mackay's death. Miss Brown was dreadfully upset. I never saw her so put out. She shut herself up in her room for two whole days afterwards and would speak to nobody. And even after that she could hardly bear to hear it spoken of.''

''And the master?'' enquired Clara, after waiting in vain for Mrs. Greenaway to go on. ''Was he distressed?''

The housekeeper did not reply directly. ''It is difficult to tell whether Mr. Mackay is distressed or not,'' she said at last. ''He is a strange gentleman but a great scholar, they say. He is not one for a word and a joke and a chat. Very moody, he can be. Not that I personally have ever had anything to complain of,'' she added hastily. ''He has always been a perfectly honourable and generous employer. So long as you do your work properly he never complains. But he is very reserved. He is not an open gentleman, if you see what I mean.''

''Perhaps,'' ventured Clara, ''he is unhappy about his wife.''

''That is very likely. It was a great tragedy to have his beautiful young wife suddenly turned into a poor pale ghost. But suffering makes some people warm and open, you know. With Mr. Mackay it was the other way. It seemed to shut him up completely. He could not even seem to find consolation in his little daughter, though he has always been very concerned about her upbringing. Nor would he entertain any society. He would never see anybody except the people in his office and some of his learned friends, and then he would never let me make a dinner for them, but they would come along and shut themselves up in his study. Oh, I nearly forgot to tell you—you are never on any account to go into the master's study. I will show you the door. He does not like to be disturbed when he is reading or writing. Mr. Benson, his manservant, sees to the cleaning and anything else that Mr. Mackay requires. Nobody else ever enters the room."

"Yes, ma'am. Yes, Mrs. Greenaway," said Clara.

But she was an observant girl, for all her timidity and inexperience, and it was not long before she noticed that the "nobody else" did not include Miss Brown. Several times she had with her own ears heard Mr. Mackay call Miss Brown into the study to show her a book or to write a letter for him, or give him her advice on something he had written.

"Certainly, Mr. Mackay," Miss Brown would say with her usual gracious little inclination of the head. "I will be with you directly."

And she would put aside whatever she was doing and walk, tall and queenly as ever, into the master's room.

Clara had the feeling that Miss Brown would rather not have gone, but did not know why she felt this. In fact the little nursemaid was puzzled by Miss Brown. The governess was always kind and even-tempered and most concerned about little Betty. You could not possibly be afraid of her, and yet at the same time you felt that you would never be really close friends with her. Perhaps it was because you felt that however amiable she was, she did not really care about you at all. She once asked about Clara's little brother and seemed to be listening when Clara told how little Bertie loved to hear tales of battles at sea and

wanted to be a sailor when he grew up. But when Clara—
who had perhaps chattered rather too much on her favourite theme—had finished talking, Miss Brown simply smiled
in her rather superior way and said: "We will have to ask
Mr. Mackay to use his influence with the Admiralty."

Clara had felt snubbed as she had not felt when Mrs.
Greenaway scolded her for dropping the tray with the
child's breakfast one morning. In fact it was always a relief
to Clara to go down to the housekeeper's quarters. Mrs.
Greenaway's cosy gossip and cups of tea, her cat and her
canary, her beadwork and her treasured photograph of her
long-dead husband, all provided a warmth and a human
interest that was to be found nowhere else in the grand
house. The child's bedroom and nursery, for all the dainty
furnishing and expensive toys, were sad places in comparison. Clara did her best, by playing games with Betty and
telling her all the tales she knew, to bring a little gaiety
into the child's life, but it was very uphill work; and somehow Miss Brown, although she gave Betty her lessons and
watched carefully over her diet and her exercise, did not
add to the fun.

The master also watched over Miss Betty in his own
way and every evening Clara had to bring the child into
the great drawing-room to greet her father.

"Well, my dear, and what have you learnt in your lessons today?" he would ask.

"The principal rivers of Europe, Papa," she would reply in her frightened little voice. Or: "The story of how
William the Norman fought and conquered King Harold."

"And did you enjoy your walk? Where did you go today?" he asked next, glancing at Clara with his unhappy
brown eyes.

"Just round the squares, sir," Clara would reply, giving
a bob of a curtsy. "Miss Betty made friends with a little
span'el dog, sir." It was on the tip of her tongue, so she
told Mrs. Greenaway later, to ask whether the lonely child
might not have a little dog, a pet of her very own to love

and care for, but she could not pluck up the courage to say it. After all, it was not her place. If anyone was to suggest that the child should have a pet dog, it was Miss Brown who should do so. Besides, the master was such a formidable-looking gentleman that you were terrified of incurring his displeasure. Not that he ever actually said anything unkind; in fact sometimes Clara thought that he cared more about other people's feelings than did Miss Brown, for all her cleverness and sweetness; but he looked so stern that you felt you could not bear it if he were to reprimand you.

Nevertheless, Clara could not help but be very interested in Mr. Mackay, as the only man in the household, and she soon decided that he was indeed very much in love with Miss Brown. You could tell that by the way his dark eyes lit up when he saw her and by the smile that transformed his tragically handsome face and made you realize what a very fine man he was. It was the lady's feelings that Clara could not understand, any more than the housekeeper was able to comprehend them. Sometimes she saw Miss Brown smile at Mr. Mackay with what seemed like warmth and affection, just as she sometimes smiled at Betty and at Clara herself. But at other times Clara caught Miss Brown looking at Mr. Mackay in a very cool and speculative manner, not at all as you would look at the man with whom you were in love. And when you added to this Miss Brown's quite obvious reluctance to be alone with Mr. Mackay, you really could not help feeling that Miss Brown did not care for him at all, and was just leading him on for her own amusement, so to speak.

This was very bad. Mr. Mackay was a gentleman who ought to have a good and loving wife, after all the unhappiness he had suffered, and there must be many women who would be only too glad to fill the place, if Miss Brown did not want him herself. Why does she not seek another position if she has refused him, said the nursemaid to herself, and give somebody else a chance? Quite apart from anything else, it made for awkwardness. Clara always felt rather uncomfortable when she was in a room together with both Mr. Mackay and Miss Brown, much more so than when she paid her respects to the master alone. However did they manage, wondered Clara, sitting alone together in the drawing-room of an evening, when all the rest of the household had gone to bed and there was nobody else present to distract them from their difficult feelings about each other?

She mentioned this notion of hers to Mrs. Greenaway, but the housekeeper, conscious perhaps of having been a little indiscreet, replied sharply: "That's none of our business, child. Don't you go making up stories, now. The master and Miss Brown understand each other very well, and if she does decide to be his wife, she will do so in her own good time. There has never been anything in the least bit improper—I should never consent to work in a household where there was—and you must keep a watch on your imaginings, Clara, and be careful what you say."

But the little nursemaid, more intelligent and perhaps more honest than the older woman, was quite right in her supposition that there was great tension and awkwardness between the master and the governess.

At about ten o'clock in the evening of the day when Tom Stiles had followed the lady in black to the house in Russell Square, the curtains of the big front room on the ground floor were drawn, the gas light in the centre of the ceiling was turned low, and the main light in the room came from two reading lamps that served the occupants of the two big armchairs that stood each side of the fine Adam fireplace. Not much more than a mile away, Peter and Lucy Bond were sitting in their tiny living-room, talking together in an animated fashion, melting away the coolness that had arisen between them during the previous week, and discussing what, if anything, they ought now to do about the manuscript of A Most Mysterious Death.

In the high elegant room in Russell Square there was

no such easy companionship. It was a sombre room, more like the library of a scholar than the drawing-room of a lady, for the late Mrs. Mackay had not entered it for many years before her death, and the attempts made in the early days of her marriage to prettify it in accordance with the current fashion, had long since vanished under the intrusion of her husband's books and papers. There were no weapons or curios kept in here; only a great many books and a few china ornaments remaining from the early days. The room was cleaned regularly and the fire lit in winter, but there was no heart in it.

On the left of the carved fireplace in the big drawing-room sat the master of the house, in a deep leather-covered armchair. He had on his knees a volume of an encyclo-paedia and on his face was his habitual expression of sternness concealing all feeling. It was a fine, distinguished face, but he looked more than his forty years; the lines had grown more numerous of late, the thick hair greyer. Opposite him in a similar chair sat Miss Brown. She had exchanged her black dress for one of a pale lilac colour. Its plainness, and the simple style in which the glossy dark hair was dressed, only emphasized the beauty and intelligence of her face. As she sat reading with her cheek resting on her hand, she looked as calm and serene as a Raphael madonna. No one, from looking at her, could have had any notion of what her thoughts and feelings were; yet a third person in the room might well have sensed the tension.

The grandfather clock struck the quarter-hour, and a few minutes later Mr. Mackay raised his eyes from his book.

"What are you reading, Jessie?" he asked.

"Meredith's *Modern Love*," she replied without looking up.

The lines round his mouth deepened slightly. "Why do you have to read that now?" he asked.

"It is a great poem. You said so yourself."

"It is too full of pain."

"But very truthful." This time she did glance up at him quickly before looking back at her book. "Love between a man and a woman must always be full of pain."

"Not always." He shook his head slowly. "By no means always." And then he added on a note of anxious appeal: "Must ours be, Jessie?"

"And there are some tender moments," she said, ignoring his cry. "Listen." And she began to read in a low voice full of feeling:

Lovers beneath the singing sky of May,
They wandered once; clear as the dew on flowers;
But they fed not on the advancing hours:
Their hearts held cravings for the buried day.

"Stop it," he cried. "I don't want to hear what follows."

She took no notice of the interruption, but read on with increasing emotion:

Then each applied to each that fatal knife,
Deep questioning, which probes to endless dole.
Ah, what a dusty answer gets the soul
When hot for certainties in this our life!—"

Her voice broke off on a sob. He was instantly at her side.

"It's not us, not *us*, Jessie." He took the volume out of her hands and threw it on to the table "*Our* love will last." He knelt before her. "It will last—say it will! Give me no dusty answer, tell me you will be my wife!"

She uttered a little moan and the next moment she was in his arms, shivering and weeping uncontrollably.

"What has distressed you, my dearest?" he asked, trying to soothe her. "Have I not waited patiently for long enough? Why do you always weep when I ask you to be my wife?"

She tried to speak but failed to make a sound.

"I shall begin to fear that I no longer have your love," he said.

"Oh no, not that!" she cried. "I love you, Laurence. I love you with all my heart. I am not quite myself today. I cannot tell you why. Give me a little longer."

"Always a little longer." There was a slight coolness in his voice.

"It is only a few months since the mourning period was ended," she said.

"And yet you so often wear black."

"I like to do so. It suits me." She had calmed down now and drawn away from him and there was a touch of coquettishness in her manner. He got to his feet and returned to his chair without saying another word.

"Have you found the information you were seeking, Laurence?" she asked. "May I copy it for you? Can I be of any help?"

"Not tonight," he said wearily. "I can read no more tonight. Tomorrow, perhaps, if you will be kind enough to check through my concluding chapter."

"I will indeed. With the very greatest of pleasure. Are you not proud to think that your work is so nearly complete?"

"I might be, if I could have some other hopes."

She made no reply. Her power of simulating warmth and affection had deserted her; nothing would rise to her lips now but the truth, and that must not be spoken.

"I shall go to bed," she said. "I am very tired too."

She got up and stood behind his chair and laid first her hand and then her lips on his hair. It was easier thus, for she need not fear that he would see the expression in her eyes. He closed his own and made no response. The lines at the corners of the mouth looked deeper than ever.

Alone in her room Jessie Brown placed the candle on

the bed table, sat on the bed within its light, and opened the book that Mr. Mackay had taken out of her hands in the drawing-room. For a few minutes she stayed quite still, reading with an expressionless face the verses telling so vividly of passion gone sour, of the dreadful withering of love. Then she flung the book away from her with an impatient cry, saying to herself: you are right, Laurence, I ought to read something more cheerful. And you are right, too, Mr. Meredith, you know it all. "A kiss is but a kiss now, and no wave of a great flood that whirls me to the sea." Oh yes, you know all about it and you were no help to me whatsoever.

She stood up and walked restlessly around the shadowy room, gently beating one hand against the other and murmuring to herself. And then, moving automatically like a sleepwalker, she picked up the candle, carried it over to the dressing-table that stood in front of the window, placed it to one side, pushed the hairbrushes and other toilet articles to the other side, unlocked the top drawer and took out pen and ink and a thick notebook bound in black. She seated herself on the stool, drew the candle a little nearer, dipped the pen in the ink and began to write.

10

The Lady With the Secret Reveals the Truth

"My little notebook," wrote Jessie Brown, "my only friend, for I have no other whom I dare trust—and I must go on writing now for it is my only ease—night after night, month after month, it has brought me comfort. My little notebook, I am so hopeless now, for my desires pull one way and my duty pulls another. Seek after fame, cries my heart. You, an abandoned child without a name, you a poor girl who has fought her own way and has always had to submit to others, you have the power now—the power of your pen. You are a writer. You suspected it and now it is confirmed. You can make your own name, you can be yourself, your very own, your only true self.

"But duty calls otherwise. A man has grown to love you, it says, who will look after you and has offered you his name and heart. And you once loved him too—loved him passionately. He loves you still, although you no longer feel the same. Marry him, says duty; care for the child, look after this household which has grown to depend on you. It is not so bad a fate; thousands of women would envy it. But it is not my fate. I know it.

"Oh Mr. Meredith, why did you not help me? I sought your help and all you said was 'this and this should be cut out, this and this revised—you must guarantee there is no libel—you must alter the ending—I am a publisher's reader, not a confessional or a court of law—if you want to confess you must go to a priest.' Go to a priest! As if I could! Ah, you are very clever, Mr. Meredith, but even you cannot have guessed the whole of the truth.

"Truth!"

She wrote the word, exclaiming it aloud. And then she looked up and in the shadowy light of the candle she saw a face—lips parted as if about to utter a cry, eyes wide and staring, dark with emotion. Above it were two wings of smooth dark hair; below it was a white lace collar resting against pale lilac. As she stared into the mirror the tension eased, the muscles relaxed, and the smooth calm mask returned. If Laurence could see how I look when I write, he would no longer love me, she thought. And then she picked up the pen again.

"Truth. Yes, you have helped me after all, Mr. Meredith. You said 'be truthful,' and I am going to try. But where shall I begin? At the very beginning, of course. My name is Jessie Brown and I was born twenty-eight years ago this month of May. So I was told, and yet it may not be the truth. I shall never know who my parents were, nor my real date of birth, nor my real name, if indeed I ever had one. They gave me a name and a birthday when they christened me. I was brought up in a foundling home, you see. I was left in the garden, on the grass beneath a cherrytree. It was blossom time, and the young maid who found me brushed the white petals from my face. Her name was Jessie, so they called me after her. And as for Brown, why, they already had a Jessie White and a Jessie Black in the orphanage, so they called me Jessie Brown. What's in a name? It has served me well enough for all these years."

Again she rested her pen and stared into the mirror, but this time no longer seeing the face.

"It was not a bad orphanage," she wrote after a while. "We had enough to eat and warm clothes in winter and though we worked hard and rules were strict, we were never actually badly treated. And little Jessie always loved me. She looked on me as her very own, her own discovery. Whenever she could she would save little tidbits from the kitchen and bring them to me. Dear good simple Jessie; she was very kind to me. And so were the good ladies who ran the home, in their own way. When they saw that I was quick at my lessons and eager to learn they did their very best for me. Most of the girls were to go into service—and we learnt enough of the domestic arts at the orphanage, God knows—but they took extra trouble with me. They taught me all they knew of history and geography and drawing and music, and one of them was a bit of a scholar, and she made me acquainted with the works of the philosophers and the great poets and encouraged me to read for myself. They really did care about giving me a start in life. They were good to me—to me, nobody's child.''

Tears rose to her eyes and she brushed them impatiently aside before continuing to write.

''I was to become a governess. They had given me equipment enough. I was sad to leave my friends in a way, but eager to go out into the world, to seek wider horizons. My first post was at a doctor's house in North London. It was not a very wealthy household and the salary was low, but I had to begin somewhere, and the good ladies at the orphanage fondly believed that in a doctor's household I should at least be looked after. The little boys were rough and rude, and it was very hard work, for I was expected to do much of the work of the household as well as teach the children. And the doctor's wife was jealous—oh, she was so jealous of me! I could not at first understand why. I had not known that I was beautiful: nobody had ever told me. But I was soon to learn. It was a most dreadful shock, a cruel awakening. I had met no men at all at the orphanage—only the visiting clergymen who came to hear our lessons from time to time. My knowledge came all through literature. I had the most elevated ideas of romantic love.

But the doctor had a young apprentice in the house whose ideas were very different. In the end I had to leave the post, but not before I had learned a great deal about the world and also learned to defend myself, and to pretend, pretend—always to pretend!

"I went next to a businessman's house, and then to a lawyer's. It was at the latter that I learnt enough to picture a lawyer for my novel. I stayed some years at both. The houses were comfortable—both in Kensington—the children well-behaved, the gentlemen very occupied with their professions, the wives with their social lives. I had learnt by then how to dress plainly, to keep my eyes cast down, to speak calmly and without feeling, to take the cue for my own behaviour from other people, and never to give any hint of any passion or independence in myself. My looks I could not quite conceal, but what man, however bold, would persist with such a very icy beauty? The years passed, the children grew up, day after day went by, each very like the other . . . I met people, I listened to people, I watched people. I learnt from them, but I played no active part. I was not unhappy, but there was no life in me. Is this all there is, I would often ask myself: is this all?

"And then the last of the lawyer's daughters married and he needed my services as governess no longer. He did not tell me to seek another post at once. There was even some talk of my remaining in the house as companion to his wife and secretary to them both. But I chose to go. It was a dull household, and I was tired of the neighbourhood. I thought of emigrating. Perhaps over the ocean in a new continent I might somehow come to life. I even visited the office of the Colonial Emigration Society, in Portman Square and made enquiries about the openings for a governess abroad. I had a little money saved; the good lawyer would have helped me further. He was, I must confess, a little bit too fond of me, but I had learnt by then how to control both him and myself and to arouse no suspicion in his wife. Meanwhile I answered advertisements, and among them was the one inserted in *The Times* by Mr. Laurence Mackay. 'A gentleman employed in Her Majesty's Service and residing in Bloomsbury seeks the services of a nursery governess to attend to the education and overall supervision of his five-year-old daughter. A nursemaid is employed, but some knowledge of nursing would be useful, since it would be appreciated if the successful applicant would be willing to attend from time to time upon the child's invalid mother.' It was the 'would be appreciated' that drew my attention. Why did it not state 'will be required to?' It is for the employer to lay down terms, not the applicant. There are always more governesses seeking for posts than there are posts to be filled. But when I came to know him I understood, for he was more considerate of his servants even than the kind lawyer had been. If ever a tender loving heart beat beneath a stern and unbending exterior! Oh, if I could but love him as I used to love him!

"But I am racing too far ahead. Let me remember that interview. It was a dull autumn day, late afternoon, and the mist was swirling round the trees in the square. I knew as soon as I saw the house that therein lay my fate.

"Now wait a moment, Jessie. Did you know? Is that true? You have sworn to write nothing but the truth, remember. Yes, Mr. Meredith, I promise you that all in this account so far is true. I must strike that sentence out. I did not know it as soon as I saw the house. It is my imagination carrying me away again into a story. I did not know it till a little later, when I faced him in the study. At the time when I looked at the house I was conscious only of being tired and cold and wanting the interview to be over. But when I first saw Laurence, I knew it then. It was not only because he was so handsome, for all his serious manner; nor that he was intelligent and interesting in his discourse, and somehow different from the others whom I had seen. All that was important, of course. I thought: here is a man I should like to get to know. We talked of his great interest—African tribal customs—and of the collection of items in his study. It was fascinating to me. It was a new sort of knowledge, something I had never come across before. And we spoke a little of music, art and poetry. We even mentioned you, yes, you, Mr. Meredith! 'A fine poet, very little known,' he said. 'A poet who sees very clearly into the human heart.' He told me he was a member of the Shelley Society and had also joined the recently formed Browning Society. He liked to talk with the sort of people he came across at their meetings.

"And he told me, of course, of the tragedy of his wife and of his worse than motherless daughter. We talked a long time, getting to know each other, though he was very formal and polite, and I was as calm and modest-seeming as I had schooled myself to be. I wanted to take the post if offered me, but I was a little afraid. It was as if I was putting my feet upon a path that led I knew not where. Then we rose to our feet as of one accord, the interview over, and his eyes sought mine with a look of appeal that seemed to turn my limbs to water. He felt as I did: I could see it. We had somehow, through our talk about African tribes and invalids and poetry, each struck some spark in the other that would not be extinguished.

"And so it all began. But you know all that, Mr. Meredith. You have read it all in my book. It is all true, except the place and the names and the profession. All to do with our feelings, all that really mattered—that is true. We drew closer and closer; we declared our love for each other. We talked about if his wife should die. Yes, yes, yes! We were very guilty, very guilty. I make no excuse. That was how it was, that was what we did. We heard the doctor declare her to be growing weaker. A shock would kill her, he said. And it would take very little to shock her. That was said over and over again. 'Do you know,' I said to him one day, 'that I had quite a shock myself when I first came into your study and saw some of those masks—they gave me quite a fright, as if I had come unexpectedly upon a skeleton. Now I am quite accustomed to them, of course, and they no longer trouble me.' 'Poor Jessie,' he replied with a smile. 'I am sorry that I frightened you. I am so used to them myself that I never think of them at all.' 'Did Louisa ever see them?' I asked. 'Even when she was well, I am sure she must have disliked them.' 'She did dislike them,' he admitted, 'she would never come into my study. God knows what it would do to her now.' 'It would kill her for sure,' I replied. 'That is the very worst of her imaginary terrors—the worst horror of her poor failing mind, that savages will come and get her.'

'This was how we talked. This was the seed from which the tale sprang. A very ordinary conversation. We had had many such. We often talked of Louisa. She clung to me. It was because I was calm and unemotional, I think. She trusted me because I was a comparative stranger to her; I was unconnected with all those people and things that had caused her illness. I had great pity for her. Yes! I did! That is true. I pitied her, even while I loved her husband. And I had pity for him too. But I did wrong. I do not excuse myself. And so did he.

"And now I must be very, very careful to write the truth of what comes next."

She put down her pen, rested her chin on her hand, and stared unseeing at her reflection in the mirror. Then suddenly the eyes in the mirror took on their dark and frightened look again and the lips parted. She exclaimed aloud: "But what is the truth? What really happened? How much is due to the imagination that created the story in my book? Which is which? Which is reality? Which is the story?"

She stared at her staring image.

"Good God, I can no longer distinguish between them! God help me, God forgive me, I no longer know which is the truth!"

She covered her face with her hands and sat there for a

few minutes rigid and motionless. Then she picked up the pen again and wrote very firmly:

"I have lived for so long in the blazing light of my story that I am no longer sure what really happened. Was it as it is in the novel? Or did I perhaps one night have a terrible nightmare, after one of our talks about the masks, and that very same night find Louisa dead of shock? The idea was in our minds—in both our minds. Did I see it in my sleep because I had willed it to be so? Or did he really come? The guilt was there. We felt it, both, although we never spoke of it. The burden of guilt was too great; and I had then, although I did not know it, already begun to love him less. Perhaps I was more in love with love, in love with excitement and passion and life, than I ever was in love with him.

"That is true, I think. Oh God, what am I! What sort of wicked creature am I? What have I done? What devils have I unleashed? If I have wronged Laurence—wronged him so grievously!"

She dropped the pen, held her face in her hands, and wept a little before she began to write again.

"I must not shrink. I cannot turn back now. I have sworn to write the truth. I have wronged Laurence—doubly wronged him. I have portrayed him as a murderer in fact, when the crime was probably only in his mind, and I have ceased to love him. Had I truly loved him, I could not have portrayed him so—I could not have written the book at all. And the book came to mean everything in life to me—more than Laurence had ever meant. I could love him, or I could write about him, but I could not do both. That is true, is it not, Mr. Meredith?

"But while I wrote I still pretended to love him. We must be careful, I said; the period of mourning is not over. He consented. He believed that when the time came I would be his. But all I was thinking was: I have so-and-so-many months left in which to finish my book. Oh, we were oceans apart! And what shall I do now? If I marry him, I become mistress of this house that already acknowledges my rule, mother to Betty who so badly needs a mother, helpmeet to my husband in all things, supporting him in all things, putting his needs always before my own, his writing before mine.

"No! That last I cannot do. The duties I could perform. I could even, if I acted with all my heart and mind, still pretend to love. But my writing I cannot give up, and neither can I tell him, never, even if I come to write tales that in no way portray himself. For he will be too jealous. He will never bear it. I know him so well. He loves to sharpen his ideas upon a woman who has brains enough to be a grindstone, and he loves a woman who can sincerely echo his own appreciation of great thoughts and great works. But for a woman to vie with him and perhaps even to excel him—and worst of all, that woman his own wife—no, never, never, never! He would pretend not to mind; he would even offer encouragement and advice—a pat on the head for a little performing dog. But every difficulty would be put in my way. I should not have one moment's true imaginative freedom. He would look hurt when I mentioned my own writing; he would tell me that Betty was longing to see more of me; he would complain that the household did not run smoothly.

"If I marry Laurence I must continue to write in secret. Would that be possible? Can two human beings live in marriage together with one holding so great a secret from the other? And if I do not marry Laurence?"

She laid down her pen and sat staring into the mirror for a long time, her hands folded under her chin, before she began to write again.

"If I do not marry Laurence it will still not be the end of life for him. He loves me very much but he will recover in time. He will find another wife, more suited to his needs; the household a mistress, poor little Betty a mother. And I? What will happen to me? Another post—like that with the lawyer perhaps? The same dull round, made worse by the emptiness after having once known passion. Ah, but I could

write! Secretly as I have written here, so long as my duties
were not too heavy and I had privacy enough. Secretly at
first and then perhaps one day, if I were really to become
famous, I would dare to declare myself and be myself—Jessie
Brown, no paid and humble servant, no man's wife or ap-
pendage, but a woman in her own right.

"Is that what I want? Yes, yes, yes, Mr. Meredith. That
is what I want and I will pay the price, whatever it may
be. And I will put aside my novel and write on another
theme. You were quite right about that, it is much too
risky, and the ending is very bad. But I already have my
theme! I will start where I am now, with what ought to
have been the ending of the other book. I will start with
a woman who finds that she is a writer and decides to give
up love itself in order to follow her vocation. Ah! I see
already how it will be—a good man, a kindly, affectionate,
but narrow sort of man—one who would confine her life
and spirit within his own limited imagination. Yes, there
is the conflict, there is to be the tension between characters
that generates the electricity that sparks off the story. The
woman will be myself, of course. The man will not be Laurence, though. Nobody at all like Laurence, and then it cannot
hurt him if he should ever read it. But who shall the man be
like? Ah, my good old lawyer friend, of course, but as a
much younger man. And he will be a doctor. Yes, I can do
that. I can see them—oh, how clearly I can see them!"

The candle burnt low. Jessie Brown got up to find another. Many hours later she laid down her pen at last,
placed the notebook at the back of the drawer of the
dressing-table and turned the key and dropped it into a
little china vase. Then she extinguished the light and lay
down, still fully clothed, on her bed. It was already dawn.
She watched the furniture in the room take on firmer out-
lines in the increasing light of day, and said to herself: I
can do it, I can write on another theme. That means I am
a real writer, does it not, Mr. Meredith?

— *11* —

I Must Recover That Manuscript!

Clara was rather disappointed when Miss Brown said she had a bad headache and would not come down to breakfast. It was another fine day, and she had hoped they might make the promised visit to the Zoo. Betty was disappointed too, and Clara blamed herself for raising the child's hopes. However, no doubt they would go another day, for Miss Brown always kept her promises, and there was no doubt that she was feeling very ill. She looked very pale and drawn as she sat on the low chair with the buttoned back, wearing a loose dressing-gown and with her black hair falling about her face. The master was so anxious about her that he actually went upstairs to see for himself how she was before he departed as usual at about ten o'clock for his office. Clara longed to know what they said to each other on this occasion, and whether they were still as awkward together, but she was of course very occupied with little Betty, and in any case she would never deign to listen at a door.

In fact she would not have learnt very much from the conversation had she heard it.

"I hear you have a headache," said Laurence Mackay after being bidden to come in in response to his knock.

"Yes," said Jessie, placing on the table by her chair the cup of tea from which she had been sipping, and staring out of the window at the tops of the plane trees in the square. They were bright with young green leaves, and still ungrimed from city dirt.

"I am very sorry. I hope you will soon feel better."

He looked concerned, but his voice was very formal.

She turned to him then and smiled faintly. "They usually last only a few hours. I shall rest this morning and be myself again, I hope, this afternoon. Is there anything that I can do for you then? Would you like me to read the final chapter of your book and check the footnotes?"

It cost her a great effort to say this. Her head was indeed aching quite badly, but it had ached much more on previous occasions and she had carried on with her duties without even mentioning it. She was deliberately using it as an excuse to soften or cover up her complete withdrawal from him, her immersion into her own world of creation that could not, at this moment, endure the intruding presence of another human creature.

"I will not trouble you," he replied. "I can see you are not well enough. There is not very much to be done to the book and I will attend to it myself this evening."

With another formal hope for her speedy recovery he bowed and left the room. She rested her head against the back of the chair and relaxed into relief. He remained in her thoughts for only a very few minutes after he had left the room. I will sleep for a few hours, she said to herself, for I can sleep now. And then I will ask Mrs. Greenaway for a light lunch, and tell Clara to take Betty for her walk, because my head is still aching badly, and I will ask not to be disturbed. And Laurence will not be home until six o'clock, so I shall have four hours—four hours in which to write in peace. I can make good progress with my story in four hours—and by daylight instead of candlelight. That will make it much easier and my head will not ache so.

With this happy prospect in mind, Jessie fell soundly asleep and remained so for most of the morning. When she awoke, refreshed, it occurred to her that she ought perhaps to do something about the manuscript of *A Most Mysterious Death* which she had flung down on the desk of the inner office at Messrs. Chapman and Hall at a moment when she was overcome with frustration and despair. I must tell them that I no longer want it to be published either with or without an amended ending, she said to herself; it was madness ever to offer it in the first place, but it has served its purpose. It taught me that I could write, and it gained me the high opinion of Mr. Meredith, and he has helped me to go on, because it was not sympathy that I needed, although I thought I did; it was a challenge, and that he has given me. Should I write to the firm now, and tell them that the book is no longer on offer?

For a moment or two she considered doing this, and then she decided that the matter was not so very pressing. Nothing would be done about the manuscript unless she agreed to revise it; Mr. Meredith had said they would certainly not publish it as it stood, and it would be safer lying in the offices of Messrs. Chapman and Hall, where nobody knew who she really was, than it would be in Russell Square. She did not want to be troubled any more with locking it away from all eyes in the house except her own; she had lost all interest in this earlier novel; the new one, to be entitled *The Price She Paid*, was absorbing all her thoughts and all her heart, and she was longing to get on with it without another moment's delay.

The day went by. Laurence returned from his office earlier than expected, looking very unhappy and locked up in his own thoughts. Jessie contrived that he and the child and herself should have a little meal together. She had not seen Betty all day, she said; it would soon be the child's bedtime, and in any case she, Jessie, did not feel up to any dinner. She escaped back to her room. Laurence dined alone, shut himself up in his study, made a few amendments to the now completed manuscript of his *History of Tribal Customs in Africa*, placed the chapters together in a neat pile, and laid a letter on top of it. The letter was dated the previous day; the address at the head was II Henrietta Street, Covent Garden; the handwriting was that of Mr. James Goodbody, and its contents were to the effect that Mr. Frederic Chapman would be delighted if Mr. Laurence Mackay would call upon him in his office at twelve noon on Friday, the 23rd of May, in order to discuss the publication of his work. It was a very courteous and interested letter. ''We are anxious to build up a list of books on travel and exploration and natural history,'' it concluded; ''you may have noticed that we have published a number of such works in recent years.''

The next morning Jessie came down to eat her breakfast with Laurence. She had made excellent progress with *The Price She Paid* and her mind was temporarily at ease. The next part of the book was still in the distance, gently beckoning to her; it had not yet become a great raging torrent in her mind, giving her no respite until it had taken the form of words on paper. For the time being, at least, she felt more capable of behaving like her former self.

''I am so sorry, dear Laurence,'' she said, ''that I was able to be of so little use to you yesterday. I did indeed feel very ill. But perhaps I can be of assistance today. What is it that you would like me to do?''

''Nothing, my dear,'' he replied looking at her with sad resignation. ''I have done all that need be. At noon today I shall be seeing the gentleman who I hope will publish my book.''

''At noon? Shall you not be in your office at that hour?''

''My dear, I am not a junior clerk. I am in charge of the Department.''

''I am sorry, Laurence. I did not mean to suggest—I mean I understood you to say you were particularly busy at the moment—I mean—''

Jessie floundered about for several moments, excusing herself and trying to stifle an alarming thought that had suddenly shot into her mind.

''I do not recollect,'' she said eventually, making a great

effort to keep her voice under control, "that I wrote any letter to any particular publisher on your behalf."

"You did not. The arrangement was made at the Club. I was talking to a man who reviews books in the *Fortnightly Review*. He suggested a firm of publishers who are making a specialty of books on travel and foreign customs and whose literary adviser is, oddly enough, none other than George Meredith. I did not know that he engaged in work of this kind. It is not generally known, I believe. I understand that he is himself very interested in studies such as my own, so I have no doubt that I shall get a fair reading."

"That is good, Laurence," said Jessie, clutching the table leg under the cloth with both her hands in order to save herself from collapsing. "I am very glad to hear it," she added faintly.

"What is the matter, my dear? Do you still feel unwell?"

There was concern, but not the least hint of suspicion in his voice. How could there be, she said to herself angrily; take a grip on yourself, Jessie Brown. This is most unfortunate, but not so very surprising. The world of publishing is a small world; it was foolish of me not to think of the possibility that Laurence might approach the same publisher as myself. And after all, what can possibly happen? It must be Mr. Chapman whom he is to see, and not Mr. Meredith. Mr. Meredith only comes in once a week, the office boy said, so I have plenty of time to write to him and explain it all and beg him to say no word about *A Most Mysterious Death* when he meets Laurence. He would not do so in any case, I am sure—why should he?—but I shall feel more at ease if I write to him. And I will ask him to keep the manuscript safe for me. Surely he will not mind doing that.

Aloud she said: "I still have a trace of headache, but I am determined to go out and enjoy the sunshine today. That will soon cure it. And at twelve noon I shall think of you talking about your book in the offices of—'' She caught herself up with a little gasp: she had very nearly said ''Chapman and Hall,'' but Laurence had not mentioned the name of the firm, so how could she be supposed to know it? They had up till now talked about the publication of his book only in the most general terms and always as if it was a distant event. She had not realized that he was in quite such a hurry, or she might have been more on her guard.

''Which firm is it,'' she asked, controlling herself with an even greater effort than before, ''that you are going to?''

''Chapman and Hall. Publishers of Charles Dickens,'' he replied. ''I shall see the Managing Director, Mr. Frederic Chapman.''

''Oh yes,'' she said brightly. ''Oh yes, I recollect. You could not do better, could you, than approach the publishers of Charles Dickens.''

After he left the house she went up to her room and sat down and cried from sheer weakness and shock. What a dreadfully narrow escape she had had from giving herself away, and how on earth was she to go on pretending now? It had been difficult enough when it was simply a matter of concealing her own writing from Laurence, but how on earth was she to keep up the pretence that she knew nothing of the publishing firm except what Laurence had told her? It was not even as if his visit today would be the end of it, so that she need only keep a guard on her tongue for a short while. No. The publication of a book lasted several months, and then there would be all the interest aroused in it. Laurence would be in frequent touch with his publishers for an indefinite period and she would never feel safe for one moment. Why, he might even become friendly with Mr. Chapman himself—or even—horror of horrors!—become friends with Mr. Meredith.

The moment Jessie thought of this she realized how very likely it was, likely not only in her imagination, but in reality. Mr. Meredith would read Mr. Mackay's book and would most certainly want to meet the author, because the subject interested him. And Laurence would be delighted to become friendly with Mr. Meredith, whom he had once met briefly, and whose writing he admired so much. The two men would take to each other at once; Jessie had no doubt of that. They had similar interests and tastes, a similarity in character—an apparent hardness concealing a lot of unhappiness underneath. Laurence would offer to show Mr. Meredith his collection, and Mr. Meredith, having just the sort of enquiring mind that wanted to know about other men's hobbies, would certainly accept, and then . . .

"But he would have guessed by then!" cried Jessie aloud, getting up and roaming about the room as if the very movement would make her thoughts more endurable. He will guess long before then that Laurence is the Henry Windlesham of my novel; he who saw at once that the novel was largely drawn straight from my life will not fail to recognize this. And in the book Henry Windlesham is a murderer! Does Mr. Meredith know that I am now far from sure myself that this is true? What will he think when he meets Laurence? Oh God, if I could but prevent their meeting! How can I, how can I?

She sat down again and tried to take a grip on her racing thoughts. I must write to Mr. Meredith, she said to herself, and tell him the whole truth; that is the only answer. But I do not have his address: how shall I procure it? Oh, if only I had told him when I had the chance! Why did I not do so? But it is not too late, because Laurence is only to see Mr. Chapman today, and Mr. Chapman is not, I believe, so likely to make connections and to suspect . . . Besides, I do not even know that Mr. Chapman has read my novel. And after all, Laurence suspects nothing so far . . . But does Laurence suspect nothing? she thought with a fresh wave of alarm; he has been much more secretive with me than I expected, he knows only too well that

I am growing cool to him. And suppose Mr. Chapman should mention to him a fascinating story that has been brought in by a young lady dressed in black who wished to remain anonymous, and tells him something about the story!

At this point in her thoughts panic overwhelmed her completely. She leapt to her feet again and cried aloud in alarm: "I must get that manuscript back and destroy it. I must fetch it immediately, with no further delay."

She prepared herself to go out and told Mrs. Greenaway and Clara that she was going shopping. The fresh air would do her good, and she would give Betty her lessons later in the day. They tried to dissuade her. She really did look very ill, she was not fit to go alone.

"The fresh air will do me good, do me good," she repeated almost hysterically.

Once out of doors she did indeed feel able to breathe more freely. The careless, impersonal bustle of the London streets came as a relief after the oppressiveness of the house. Yet again she made her way down Drury Lane and Long Acre, and negotiated the crowded, noisy roadways of Covent Garden market. Only when she was in Henrietta Street did it occur to her that she was not wearing black, as on her previous visits to the publisher's office, and, even worse, had no veil. The tip-tilted little hat that was her usual style of head-covering fully revealed her face. However, it was too late to do anything about that now. It was already dangerously near to the time when Laurence himself would be arriving in the neighbourhood. And in any case, she tried to comfort herself, she would see only the office boy and the clerks, and they would be most unlikely ever to go to meetings of the Shelley Society or anywhere else where they might recognize her.

She straightened her shoulders, threw back her head and for the third time pushed open the front door of Messrs. Chapman and Hall, publishers.

12

A Young Clerk Plays His Part

"Crikey!" exclaimed Tom, as he heard the street door open. "Not another caller!"

The office was very busy that morning. Changes in the Board of Directors were being planned, and two gentlemen were at that very moment closeted with Mr. Chapman to discuss the matter. Mr. Goodbody was rushing about like a distracted hen, and clerks from the Trade Department and the Counting House kept turning up with bits of information that they said Mr. Chapman had asked for. In addition to that, the representatives came in on Fridays to hand in their weekly reports on sales, and some nincompoop had gone and booked Mr. Chapman to interview a prospective author at twelve o'clock, instead of leaving it over until a less busy day. Everyone denied doing this, but at the same time most of the clerks had their own suspicions as to the culprit. It was also known that Mr. Chapman was particularly keen to get away from the office early that afternoon, as there was to be a cricket match played near his home on the following day, and he had a whole lot of people coming to stay at his house at Banstead to celebrate the event.

Tom himself was behindhand with his work. It was one of his tasks to keep up to date the big ledger in which were recorded the full names and titles and addresses of all the individuals and organizations with which the firm had to deal, but he had been so busy with all the comings and goings and showing people upstairs and running errands for Mr. Chapman that he still had a pile of letters and copies of letters and odd slips of paper containing information that was to be entered into the address book. Neither had he yet had the chance, with all the rush that had been going on yesterday and this morning, to tell his friend Peter Bond the great secret that he had found out where the lady in black lived.

He got down from his stool for about the twentieth time in the last hour, somewhat reluctantly. He liked to have plenty going on, but this was getting a bit too much. He would never finish his writing work at this rate, and old Goodbody would be nagging him again. A tall young woman dressed in pale lilac and with a little straw hat perched on top of her thick glossy black hair, confronted him. Tom goggled at her.

"You do not recognize me, Tom," she said with a flicker of a smile lighting up her rather worried-looking face. "Miss Faith Freeman. I have come about my manuscript—*A Most Mysterious Death*."

Tom took a grip on himself. "Oh yes, ma'am? What can I do for you?"

"I had a slight misunderstanding," she said hurriedly, "with your reader when he was kind enough to give me some advice. I was foolish enough to take offence, but I have thought better of it now and I will take the manuscript away and do what he asks. Could you please fetch it for me?"

Her voice had gathered confidence as she spoke, but her whole manner betrayed intense anxiety.

Tom stuck his pen behind his ear and scratched his head. "I don't rightly know, ma'am," he began. This was a poser. Manuscripts were very important things, and even small decisions about them should not be taken by the office boy, not even for the sake of a very beautiful lady who was no longer dressed in black. "I have no instructions," he continued uncertainly.

"But it is my own work!" she cried, and he saw a flash of fury in the fine dark eyes. "It belongs to me. Your reader would have handed it back to me, but I was foolish enough to let it fall. Please fetch it for me at once!" she concluded imperiously.

To Tom's immense relief, at that moment Peter Bond came into the room and was at once appealed to. Peter was himself looking very worried and pale, as if he were short of sleep.

"You say that our reader suggested you should take the manuscript away and revise it?" he asked.

"Yes, yes," she cried impatiently. "I was to alter the ending."

"In that case," said Peter slowly, "there can hardly be any objection to—" He broke off, thought for a moment, and added with a hint of suspicion: "Then why did you not take it with you, madam, if that was what was arranged?"

"I have explained," cried the visitor, "that I was very stupidly offended at the suggestion that I should re-write my work, and I left the manuscript on the desk. I have now thought it over calmly and I see that your reader was perfectly right. I should like to set to work at once on the revision. That is the full story. And now may I please have my book. I left it lying on the desk in the little room upstairs."

Peter turned to Tom. "Go up, will you, and see if it is still there."

There was a tense and awkward silence in the office while Tom was absent on this errand. The visitor stood tapping nervously on the floor with her parasol, and the clerk surveyed her full beauty without being moved by it. Peter Bond had no very kindly feelings towards the author of *A Most Mysterious Death*. From her account of her own character in the book, he judged her to be a dangerous woman, and she had, among other things, been the cause of an unpleasant coolness between himself and his beloved Lucy. This was now, thank God, at an end, but it had been very disagreeable while it lasted. Fortunately Lucy had believed him the other night when he told her that he really had tried to catch Mr.

Meredith and tell him of their suspicions; she had believed him when he had told her that they had been so desperately busy all yesterday that he had no chance to say anything to Mr. Chapman; she trusted him now to tell Mr. Meredith or Mr. Chapman the moment he could possibly do so, and she had promised to take no actions on her own account meanwhile. So all was now happy between them again, but no thanks to the lady who wrote under the pen name of Faith Freeman, and he still had the tiresome duty to carry out, of passing on Lucy's own story.

Meanwhile Peter was by no means sure that he was doing right in handing back the manuscript, but there was nobody else present to take a decision. Mr. Meredith was at his home at Box Hill; Mr. Chapman was discussing matters of great importance to the future of the firm and it was as much as anyone's life was worth to interrupt him; Mr. Goodbody, even if he were not rushing in and out of Mr. Chapman's office like a crazy creature, would be useless in any case when it came to exercising his own judgement; and as for the rest of the clerks who were concerned with manuscripts, they would be only too willing to pass the responsibility back to him. Well, if he was doing wrong, he would simply have to bear the consequences. Even Lucy could not accuse him of lack of decision in this matter. If Mr. Chapman dismissed him, then he would simply have to look for another post. But he did not really, in his heart, feel that it would come to that. Mr. Chapman might storm and swear, but when it came to the point, Mr. Meredith would see him through.

Nevertheless, this was a very critical moment for a young man who was nervous of taking responsibility, and it was with a great, though rather shamed, feeling of relief that Peter heard Tom say on his return that he could not find the manuscript of *A Most Mysterious Death* in the little room upstairs.

"Then our reader will have taken it away with him," said Peter. "I am very sorry, madam, but I am afraid we cannot help you. I will inform our reader of your visit and ask him what is to be done. No doubt he will write to you about the manuscript."

"Too late!" It burst from her irrepressibly. There was a look of something like panic in her eyes. "Are you quite sure that your reader has taken it away?" she cried. "Are you quite sure that the manuscript is not still in the office somewhere?"

Peter and Tom exchanged looks. They both had a big backlog of work to do, and the moment the present conference upstairs was ended, a great deal more would come flooding out at them. The last thing they wanted to do was to waste time looking for a manuscript that they felt quite sure Mr. Meredith had taken away with him. And if he had not, then he would have left if on Mr. Chapman's desk for Mr. Chapman to deal with, and they would as soon enter a cage full of hungry lions as go into Mr. Chapman's room at this moment. Even Tom, admirer of the lovely author though he was, wished that she would go away and let them get on with their work.

"It is on one of the desks, perhaps," she said, "and you have all been so busy that you overlooked it."

She was moving eagerly around the room as she spoke, peering up on to a shelf, trying the handle of a cupboard door. This was the limit. Even Tom thought so, and Peter found his rare anger rising.

"It is not in this room, madam, I do assure you," he said.

She sensed the coolness in the usually gentle voice and gave a little moan of despair.

"Oh, I do so want it now!" she cried.

Again Peter and Tom exchanged looks, and as if by unspoken agreement they began to make a pretence of looking for the manuscript among the papers on the desks and in the cupboards. She followed their movements like an eagle-eyed housewife watching an inexperienced housemaid.

"Could it perhaps be in Mr. Chapman's room?" she asked at one point."

"No, madam, it would certainly not be there," said Peter firmly, surprising even himself by this unexpected capacity to lie, and earning an even more surprised look from Tom, which fortunately the visitor did not notice. "Our reader will have taken it home, I have no doubt of it," added Peter.

"Then perhaps you will kindly give me your reader's address so that I may write to him myself," she said.

"I am very sorry, madam, but we are not allowed to do that," replied Peter without hesitation. This was a not uncommon request from authors, and he felt on perfectly firm ground in refusing it. "If you would care to leave a letter for him it will be forwarded," he said.

The visitor thought for a moment. This was not very much, she was saying to herself, but it was better than nothing. Time was flying and it was not safe to remain here much longer.

"But I have no writing materials," she said, looking so dejected for all her light clothing and smart little hat that Tom, remembering how she had sat in St. Paul's churchyard and sobbed as if her heart would break, was moved afresh. If Peter had not been there to keep him on the side of common sense, he really believed that he would have gone up to Mr. Chapman's room, or even given her Mr. Meredith's name and address against all instructions and in spite of the wrath that it would bring down upon him. As it was, all that he could do was produce pen and paper for her, and Peter rather ungraciously made room for her to sit at his desk.

Dear Sir [she wrote in such agitation that her normally clear writing was well-nigh illegible], I must see you urgently. An unexpected matter has arisen—I am in the utmost distress and I must have your help. My whole future and that of others is at stake. Let me know at once where and when I may speak with you. I shall haunt the Post Office until I find your reply. It is as a writer and not as a woman that I appeal to you. You cannot ignore the plea of a writer—and that I am a writer is beyond doubt. I have proved it since I saw you—Yours ever gratefully, Faith Freeman.

She did not read it through; she scarcely realized what she was writing: she had even begun to sign her real name and had had to alter the "J" of Jessie into the "F" of Faith. She folded the paper, placed it in an envelope, sealed it, and wrote "For Chapman's Reader" at the top. Then she stood up and said in such an unhappy voice that Tom's heart was moved afresh: "Should I not pay you for the postage? I have no stamp with me, but—"

She made as if to take out a coin from her purse.

"There is no need," said Peter. "We will put this with the other papers to go to our reader."

"And it will not be lost?" Her voice was still very anxious, but there was also that note of arrogance again.

"It will not be lost, madam," said Peter coldly.

"Nor seen by any other eyes than those for whom it is intended?"

Peter's reply to this was an indignant: "Madam!" and Tom, after his momentary weakening, began to feel impatient with her again.

A clattering sound came from just outside the window, as if some sort of vehicle was drawing up at the street door. With a little cry of alarm, and without even saying "Thank you" or "Goodbye," the visitor rushed out of the room.

The young man and the boy stared at her retreating figure, and then they stared at each other, shrugged their shoulders, and let out deep breaths. There really was not anything they could say. By unspoken consent, they moved to their desks and hurriedly began to write again. The peace lasted only five minutes, and then the expected invasion began. Mr. Chapman, the two gentlemen he had been in conference with, and Mr. James Goodbody all crowded into the office together, pouring out a flood of instructions, calling for cabs, calling for letters to be posted, other members of staff to be summoned, and altogether driving to distraction two already very harassed young clerks.

13

An Eminent Publisher Loses His Head

When the worst of the rush was over at last and Mr. Chapman had stumped off upstairs again, looking very glum after being reminded that a gentleman was coming to see him at twelve noon to discuss his book, Peter and Tom collapsed on to their stools, took out the sandwiches that their womenfolk at home had prepared for them, and wondered aloud whether there would be any opportunity to nip round the corner for a mug of something to drink. Mr. Goodbody had disappeared. They strongly suspected that it was on an errand not unconnected with thirst.

At precisely one minute to twelve the door opened yet again, and in came a tall, stern-looking but very handsome grey-haired gentleman. He handed a card to Tom, and while the boy was reading it, looked with an air of faint surprise around the now chaotically untidy office.

"Mr. Laurence Mackay," said Tom, hastily swallowing a crumb. "Mr. Chapman is expecting you, sir. I am to show you up directly." Yet again he climbed the steep staircase, the stern-looking gentleman following, briefcase in hand. Tom knocked on the door of the big front room, waited until he heard the gruff "Come in", held the door open and said smartly: "Mr. Mackay, sir!" The visitor walked in, Tom pulled the door to behind him, tumbled

123

rather than walked down the stairs, staggered into the office, and collapsed on to his stool again, wiping his brow.

"We ought to be safe for a few minutes now," said Peter, taking a coin from his pocket. "Just nip round the corner, Tom. I will cover for you if anything happens."

Nothing happened for a full ten minutes apart from Tom and Peter refreshing themselves. At the end of that time, to their great surprise, Mr. Frederic Chapman himself appeared in the doorway.

"I want to see Easton the moment he comes," he said in his most peremptory manner.

Robert Easton was the chief sales representative, a very important person for the well-being of the firm. He usually looked in at about half past twelve on a Friday to report progress.

"Yes, sir," said Peter promptly, trying to hide the last of his sandwiches under a letter. "Are we to send him up even if Mr. Mackay is still with you?"

"Yes. Send him up straight away. I can talk to him in the back room. Mr. Mackay understands that I may have to leave him for a few minutes. Damn silly time to book an appointment," he added in an angry mutter, with his eyes turning longingly towards the mug that stood on Peter's desk.

Peter, correctly interpreting the look, asked tentatively: "Shall I fetch you a drink, sir?"

"Yes," said Mr. Chapman gratefully, and then quickly added: "No. I'll have a bottle of port up. Here you, boy!"

Tom jumped briskly to attention.

"Go down and fetch a bottle—take it from the far end, and mind you carry it carefully!"

The last words were shouted after the already retreating Tom.

"Very exhausting day, very tiring indeed," said Mr. Chapman to the room at large.

"Yes, sir," said Peter, and then there was another rather awkward silence in the room, while Peter tried to look as if he was concentrating on his work, and Mr. Chapman tried to look as if he was not feeling guilty for leaving his visitor alone while he refreshed himself. Fortunately Tom quickly returned, carrying the bottle as tenderly and carefully as if it had been an infant in arms. Peter took a glass from a cupboard where a few were kept for just such emergencies, and Mr. Chapman, watching him, suddenly said: "You are looking pale, my poor fellow. Take a glass for yourself. It will do you good. And for the young 'un too. Never too early to get to know the flavour of a good port, eh?"

A minute later the astonished Tom found himself drinking a glass of the governor's best port, poured out for him by the governor's very own hand. Cor, he said to himself; won't Ma stare when I tell her! He felt himself to be very much a man of the world, and there floated in front of his eyes a delectable vision of a dignified and authoritative gentleman, Thomas Stiles, Esquire, Managing Director, saying with friendly condescension to the newest recruit to the staff: "You're looking tired, my poor fellow. Take a glass of port."

The dream came to an abrupt end when Mr. Chapman told him to get on with his work now, but it had been very pleasant while it lasted.

"I will take another glass, and one for Mr. Mackay. Bring them up, will you, Bond," said Mr. Chapman. He went slowly upstairs, with Peter following, and they entered the big room in procession.

Mr. Laurence Mackay, who had been leaning closely over the corner of the desk nearest to where he was seated in order to read something that lay on it, drew back with a guilty start as they came in. Neither Mr. Chapman, his mind full of a great variety of business matters, nor Peter, very occupied with the drinks, noticed this gesture. Peter withdrew, and Frederic Chapman leant back in his swivel chair with a grunt of relief and puffed a little before he spoke.

"I must beg your pardon, sir," he said, "for my great discourtesy in leaving you, and I am afraid I may have to do so again in a few minutes' time. Unfortunately you have caught me on a very busy day. I wish my clerk had thought to make this appointment for next week, when we could have talked at greater leisure and done far more justice to this fascinating work of yours."

He took out a handkerchief and wiped his face. It really was much too hot a day for a heavy programme of business. However, the job had to be done, and authors of interesting scholarly books had to be treated with consideration, especially when they also happened to be high Government officials. Mr. Chapman was perfectly sincere in saying he wished that he could discuss the manuscript on African tribes at greater leisure. It was just the sort of subject that interested him and it would interest George too. Of course the firm would be delighted to publish the book. There would not be a big sale, but it would be a steady one, and it would impress the sort of people whom one needed to impress. He was very glad that Mr. Mackay had brought the work to him, and he also liked the author himself. An unaffected, sensible sort of man, he seemed to be. A little buttoned-up, reserved perhaps, not given to expressing his feelings; but that was all to the good in a business discussion with an author. If there was one thing that Mr. Chapman disliked, it was having authors splashing their emotions all over the place. The novelists were the worst, and the ladies worst of all. He was always thankful that old George was there to deal with them.

But Mr. Laurence Mackay was an author after Mr. Frederic Chapman's own heart. Nothing was said that was not strictly relevant to the matter in hand. Price, publication date, the format of the book, the illustrations, the advance publicity—all were discussed in the most efficient and businesslike manner imaginable. Almost too efficient, Frederic Chapman thought at one point. Mr. Mackay seemed as coolly disposed towards the publication of his own book as if he was a merchant selling tons of coal. This really was rather unusual and even a trifle disconcerting. Frederic Chapman was a publisher of long standing, and even though he did not like authors indulging their own emotions, he still felt that a decent interest in the future of one's own work should be displayed. He himself was fully prepared, even in the midst of this busy day, for the normal little exchange of flattering courtesies— "great satisfaction to have my book published under your imprint, Mr. Chapman," "Not at all, sir, the honour is ours." That sort of thing.

But Mr. Laurence Mackay seemed to be interested only in concluding the business as fast as possible, and when the summons came from Mr. Chapman to attend to Mr. Easton in the back room, there was really very little left to be said except polite goodbyes.

"I have to ask you to excuse me again," said Mr. Chapman. "It will only be for a few minutes. Perhaps you would care to look at our latest volume on travel." He reached out across the crowded desk and handed a book to the visitor. "Your own book will have very much the same appearance."

Mr. Mackay took the book with a word of thanks, but as soon as Mr. Chapman had left the room he put it down and continued with his interrupted reading at the corner of the desk.

Cool sort of customer, rather a cold fish, was Mr. Chapman's slightly revised judgement of his visitor as he left the room. And while the surface of his mind was occupied with talking to his chief representative, there was a very curious sort of undercurrent going on below. African tribes, he was saying to himself; where have I been reading something quite recently that had some mention of interest in African tribes? It came to him with a sharp little click, so that he exclaimed aloud, and Mr. Easton, who had been saying nothing more startling than that he thought the new editions of the works of Thomas Carlyle were going quite well, looked up at his employer in surprise.

Mr. Chapman took a grip on both his speech and the top surface of his mind, but the undercurrent was turning into a rather disturbing stream. Nothing to do with it, he said to himself irritably: such coincidences do not occur. And in any case, we are not even sure that the wretched novel is about real people. Even George is not quite sure. I must be imagining things. Thinking too much. Trying to see through brick walls. I am getting as bad as George. In any case I shall get rid of the novel this afternoon: I wish I had sent it away yesterday.

He thanked Mr. Easton for his good work on behalf of the firm, bade him goodbye, and returned to the big front room. He was surprised to see the door standing open, and even more surprised to see that the visitor was no longer there. Mr. Goodbody, summoned from downstairs by Mr. Chapman's usual expedient of shouting through the inside window instead of using the bell, could not solve the mystery. None of them downstairs had seen the visitor go, he said; perhaps Mr. Mackay had suddenly recollected an important appointment and had slipped out quietly. Mr. Goodbody could offer no other explanation. After all, Mr. Mackay was in some high office in Government, was he not?

This last remark, to Mr. Goodbody's surprise and relief, seemed to soothe Mr. Chapman a little. A high Government official, he was saying to himself: there was something reassuringly mundane about the very ring of the words. High Government officials in real life were somehow very far removed from murderous lawyers in novels, even if there was an interest in African tribal customs in both cases. Lots of people were interested in such customs, otherwise there would be no point in publishing this book. And now to get rid of that other damned book, that potential best-seller that was no use to him, and that would only continue to be an irritant so long as it remained on his desk.

"I want you to write to the author of *A Most Mysterious Death* straight away," said Mr. Chapman.

"Yes, sir," said Mr. Goodbody smartly, with notebook and pen at the ready.

"The Merediths dined with us last night," went on Mr. Chapman, "and I promised to deal with it today without fail. Mr. Meredith was fussing about it again. Never knew him to get into such a state over a book. Can't think what's the matter with the man."

"What am I to write, sir?" asked Mr. Goodbody, as Mr. Chapman seemed to be suddenly sunk deep in thought.

"What? Eh? Oh, the usual sort of thing. No need for me to dictate it all. Tell her we confirm that our reader thinks very highly of her novel but is not satisfied with the ending. If she can revise it to our satisfaction we shall be happy to consider the manuscript again. But she must, of course, guarantee to us that the novel contains no libel on any living person. Rub that in well, James, that will frighten her off for sure."

"Yes, sir. The novel might be libellous, might it, sir?" ventured Mr. Goodbody.

"Mr. Meredith seems to think so. At any rate he says that the author nearly fainted when he told her she would have to guarantee us against libel actions. That looks like an admission of guilty knowledge, does it not, James?"

"It most certainly does, sir."

"All right. Get that off at once. There are just one or two more matters to attend to and then I shall be off myself."

"Yes, sir. May I have the manuscript please, sir?"

"The manuscript? What manuscript?"

"Of Miss Faith Freeman's *A Most Mysterious Death*."

"Oh yes. Of course. It was on my desk. George dumped it here, damn him."

It was at that point that Mr. Chapman began to show signs of losing not only his temper but also his head.

"I cannot see it, sir," said Mr. Goodbody nervously.

"It must be there. It was there this morning," was the furious reply.

"It does not seem to be here now, sir."

With a great cry of rage and alarm Mr. Chapman flung himself upon the mass of papers on his desk, scattering them wildly in all directions. Mr. Goodbody, bobbing about on the other side of the desk, fielded the flying documents as best he could. When the room was a shambles and the exhausted Mr. Goodbody could see hours of work ahead before it was reduced to anything like order again, Frederic Chapman desisted at last, sank back into his chair, and gave a great groan.

"Someone has stolen it," he said in a voice of doom.

14

And an Entire Publishing House Comes to a Halt

"Perhaps one of the staff took it downstairs," suggested Mr. Goodbody as encouragingly as he could. "I will go down and see," he added, thankful to have an excuse to escape from the room.

Mr. Chapman, slumped heavily in his swivel chair, made no reply.

But if Mr. Goodbody had hoped to find a peaceful breathing-space in which to recuperate in the office downstairs, he very soon discovered that his hopes were in vain. A little drama had been taking place there during his absence, not as violent as the one that had been enacted upstairs, but every bit as alarming in its implications. Peter, Tom, and the three other clerks who dealt with manuscripts were all huddled together round Tom's desk, staring at something that lay on it, and all talking at once.

"I tell you it is the same address! I swear it is!"

The boy's voice rung out high and clear above the babble.

"What's all this, what's going on here?" Mr. Goodbody, gaining a fresh spurt of energy from seeing the chance to exercise his authority, elbowed his way into the midst of them like an investigating police constable and grabbed Tom unceremoniously by the shoulder.

"What's all this?" he said again.

Everybody was only too anxious to tell him, but since they all spoke at once he could not understand a word.

"Shut up!" he shouted in an exasperated manner not unworthy of Mr. Chapman himself, "and give the boy a chance to speak. Now, Tom."

Tom explained hastily. For once he was really glad to see Mr. Goodbody come into the room. "It is the address book," he said. "I got behind with writing the addresses in with all the rush there has been these last days, and I have only just reached the letter from Mr. Laurence Mackay who came to see Mr. Chapman today. You left it with the others for me to copy the address into the book. It is Twenty-two Russell Square in Bloomsbury. But I know that address, Mr. Goodbody." Tom grabbed hold of the older clerk in his excitement and was not reprimanded. "It is the same address as Miss Faith Freeman—the author of *A Most Mysterious Death*."

"What?" yelled Mr. Goodbody. "How do you know her address? We write to her Poste Restante."

"I know we do." Tom took a gulp and went on. "I followed her—when she left on Wednesday after seeing Mr. Meredith. She came rushing downstairs just as I was starting out with that parcel for Regent's Park. She was in a terrible state—crying and sobbing and rushing across the street without looking where she was going. I thought she was going to run under a cart or drown herself or something like that," said Tom defensively, "and I thought I had better follow her for a while and see that she came to no harm. So I did. It was not so very much out of my way."

He looked at Mr. Goodbody with an air of defiance, convinced that this time he was going to get a scolding, but the other man was hanging on his words. "Go on, go on," he said.

"She never noticed me," continued Tom. "She stopped at a house in Russell Square. I watched from near the railings of the garden opposite. I saw a little girl with a nursemaid come towards her, and she kissed the little girl and then took out a key and they all went into the house together. It was number twenty-two, the same as Mr. Laurence Mackay's house.''

"But that is not the end." Peter Bond took over the story. "She came in this morning in great distress, asking for the manuscript back, and saying she had left it with Mr. Meredith upstairs in the back office. We told her it was no longer there—"

"And she didn't half carry on!" broke in Tom, suddenly lapsing into the speech of his childhood. "In a regular taking she was. Cor!"

"She was indeed," agreed Peter. "She would not go away till we had looked all round this room and even then she tried to look into the cupboards herself."

"The manuscript was on Mr. Chapman's desk," said Mr. Goodbody.

"Yes, but we did not know that," said Peter. "In any case, we could not have interrupted him if we had known. And there is something more. I have been trying to tell Mr. Meredith or Mr. Chapman about it for days but have never had the chance."

It was Peter's turn to be on the defensive; but Mr. Goodbody was past scolding anybody: his chief emotion was one of utter bewilderment. Peter briefly explained what *A Most Mysterious Death* was about and why his wife Lucy believed that the story might well have a lot of foundation in fact, and Mr. Goodbody's bewilderment began to give way to alarm. "But it could not have been taken by the lady herself," he said slowly, "even if she did succeed in coming back and slipping upstairs without anybody noticing her, because there has been somebody in Mr. Chapman's room the whole morning—" He broke off and his jaw dropped as the full implications of the loss of the manuscript began to dawn on him, but after a minute or two he recovered enough to tell the others that the manuscript had disappeared from Mr. Chapman's desk, and as it had been there first thing in the morning, and neither of the two gentlemen with whom Mr. Chapman had been discussing the future of the firm could have had the least interest in making off with it, there was only one person left who could be responsible, and that was the man described in the manuscript as a murderer.

Mr. Goodbody's narration was very dramatic, and he had the satisfaction of seeing his own horror reflected on all the faces around him when he had finished.

"We must tell Mr. Chapman now what you say about your wife, Peter," he concluded with a sort of gloating gloom. "And also what Tom says about the address. You had both better come up and tell him now. And you others had better start looking for the manuscript—just in case. Mr. Chapman said we were to look everywhere in the building."

They found Mr. Chapman still slumped in his chair, staring unhappily at the total disorder of papers on his desk and on the floor. Lulled into a false sense of security by his seeming apathy, Mr. Goodbody encouraged Peter and Tom to tell their tales. When they had finished, Mr. Chapman leant forward and gripped the edge of the desk. His face was purple; he looked as if he was about to have an apoplectic fit. The clerks sidled round to the far side of the big desk and huddled there, ready to duck if need be. But Mr. Chapman did not start throwing things. He got to his feet, brought his fist down with a mighty crash on the top of the desk, and exploded into thunderous speech.

"Get me George! Send him a wire at Box Hill! I don't care if he is writing fifty immortal verses, he is to come here *at once*!" And the fist came down again. "It's all his fault, God damn him! He's too clever by half. If he had not been so deucedly subtle in the first place we would never have got into this infernal fix."

And Mr. Chapman sank back into his chair, mopping

his brow. The clerks scuttled off to do his bidding, muttering to each other, when they themselves had calmed down a little, that this last accusation was rather unfair. The infernal fix that the firm was in was surely due as much to Mr. Chapman's carelessness as to Mr. Meredith's cleverness. However, Mr. Meredith was more than capable of looking after himself, and it would be a very great relief to have his protective presence in the office on what looked like being the most shattering afternoon that even the oldest of the clerks could ever remember.

"What shall I say in the wire?" asked Mr. Goodbody.

"Say it's a matter of life and death," cried Tom, jumping about excitedly, his eyes wide open, his jaw dropping again the moment he had spoken.

"It may well be that," said Peter more soberly. Perhaps because of what Lucy had told him, he was feeling alarmed in a way that the other clerks were not. They were worried, it was true, because Mr. Chapman was obviously in a tremendous stew, and it was certainly very worrying that the manuscript of *A Most Mysterious Death* had been removed from the office and was at this moment probably being read by the very man who had been pictured as the murderer in the book; but at the same time there was a certain element of enjoyment in their alarm, as if the whole thing was an exciting story that by some quirk of nature they happened to be living in instead of reading or listening to. They could not quite believe that real tragedy might result, but Peter could, and he was the most relieved of any of them when some time later a long wire came back from Mrs. Meredith, saying that her husband was at the moment visiting a neighbour but he was not expected to be gone very long and she would tell him the moment he came in and send him to catch the very first train. Why, Mr. Meredith might easily have been out on one of his long country walks and not expected back till nightfall! Whatever would Mr. Chapman have done then?

Even so, the waiting time was dreadful. Peter felt that

something ought to be done at once; somebody ought to go round to Russell Square straight away. He plucked up courage to suggest this to Mr. Chapman, but the unhappy Managing Director did not appear to hear him. He seemed to be sunk in torpor, only rousing himself every now and then to ask them to check the time-table yet again for the afternoon trains from Box Hill. Perhaps he had had some sort of a fit. He certainly looked ill enough. At one point they even wondered whether they ought to send for a doctor.

"If Mr. Chapman will not go, then cannot you go?" said Peter to Mr. Goodbody. "Could not we go together?"

Mr. Goodbody replied that far be it from him to fail to take any action that might help to spare people great distress, but he really could not see that either he alone, or he and Peter together, would be able to do anything. They would present themselves at the door of this grand mansion, two humble clerks, and would ask to see the master. Did Peter really suppose that they would be welcomed in? No servants would believe it if they said that the master had stolen a manuscript from their firm. On the contrary, they would probably be suspected of having burglarious intentions themselves. And what other story could they tell to gain themselves admittance?

Peter listened unhappily. Mr. Goodbody might or might not simply be making excuses for doing nothing, but the fact remained that everything he said was only too true. There was no hope of men in their position achieving anything by going on such an errand. It needed somebody with authority, somebody who could talk to the master of the house as an equal, someone with determination and quick wit and presence of mind. If only Mr. Meredith would come! If only Mr. Chapman would rouse himself and take some action!

The afternoon wore on. Nobody pretended to do any work. The clerks occupied themselves in looking for the manuscript of *A Most Mysterious Death*, without the least hope of ever finding it, and instructed the Trade Department and the Counting House and the packers and all the rest of the staff to do the same. The work of the entire publishing house came to a halt while people climbed up to peer on high shelves where the dust had lain undisturbed for years, broke into cupboards whose contents had not been required for so long that the keys had been lost; or turned the papers on their desks and in the drawers over and over again in a desultory manner. Urgent letters remained unwritten, cheques unsent, parcels unpacked. Only the men at the trade center, obliged by the very nature of their duties to handle some of the firm's business, and Tom, attending to a few enquiries in the front office and sending a few letters off in the post, did any work at all that afternoon.

At about half past four, when the clerks were so weary with waiting and anxiety that they had all of them, even Peter Bond, very nearly ceased to care what happened and were wondering whether perhaps a great fuss was being made about nothing at all, Tom reported that a hansom cab was pulling up at the door.

"It's him!" he cried, reporting back a moment later. "Gone straight upstairs and he don't half look in a state. Hasn't even stayed to put on his hat. I bet he had to run to catch that train!"

Some time later the clerks, crowding round the doorway, saw the two gentlemen come downstairs, presenting a very odd contrast in personal appearance to anyone who was sufficiently detached, at that moment, to observe it. One of them was top-hatted and suitably dressed in sober city clothes; the other, in light country jacket and trousers, with hair ruffled and a flowing red tie, looked as if he ought to be coming out of an artist's studio rather than an eminent publishing house. The look on their faces, however, was very much the same: a very worried look indeed.

"Call a cab at once, please," said Mr. Meredith to Tom.

Years later, when Tom Stiles, a bright and ambitious young publisher's representative, was relating the story of this extraordinary day to the young lady who had consented to be his wife, he laid particular stress on the fact that at this most tense and vital moment, Mr. Meredith had actually said "please" to him, the office boy. "Call a cab at once, please," he had said. The little detail had ingrained itself in Tom's memory. Perhaps it was because this was the last of the part that he himself played in the story. The rest of it, Tom at least, was hearsay.

And so it was for the other clerks. Most of them, had they been quite truthful, would have confessed to being extremely relieved that their part in the drama was at an end, and that the responsibility for action had been put back where it belonged, on the shoulders of their managing director and his chief advisor. Only Peter's wife Lucy admitted to being a tiny bit disappointed that she had, after all, had so very little to do with the whole business, considering that it was she who had been clever enough to see through to the truth in the first place. That someone else could claim to have done this even earlier than herself she would never admit. She had been the first to produce any evidence—real proper evidence. Mr. Meredith's hunch? No, that was not real evidence; that was just a guess, a writer's imagination running away with him. To her, Lucy, belonged the honour of first spotting that *A Most Mysterious Death* might be for the most part a true story and Peter, because he loved her, had to agree with her. As to the ending, had not she, Lucy, also said that she did not believe in the ending? Mr. Meredith was not the only person who could judge whether the end of a novel read convincingly or not. But even Lucy had to admit that she could not have forecast the real end.

15

The Pen Is Mightier . . .

When Jessie Brown left the offices of Messrs. Chapman and Hall for the last time, the thought that was uppermost in all the turmoil of her mind was annoyance with herself for failing to gain her object. In spite of what the clerks had said, she found it difficult to believe that Mr. Meredith had taken the manuscript of *A Most Mysterious Death* away with him again. Why should he? He had done his work on it. As he had said himself, he had plenty of other matters to attend to, and he had probably already given more time to it than it was customary to give to a manuscript. He would surely feel, after she had rushed away so foolishly, that he was not obliged to trouble about it any more.

What would happen to it then? This was where Jessie blamed herself. If only she had kept her head a little better just now she could have got more information out of the boy and the young man in the office. She who had grown to know so well the power of her own beauty and charm over men, and who was very experienced in exploiting these qualities, ought not to have been so easily put off by a little whipper-snapper of a lad who obviously thought she was wonderful, and by a shy-looking, modest young man who had probably never before in his life encountered anyone quite like Jessie. What she ought to have done, of course, was to be much less forthright. She should have asked them very humbly to look for the manuscript for her; she should have smiled on them in sweet apology, sympathized with them for being so busy in the office on a hot morning; really studied their state of mind and worked on it, as she did with the servants at home. At the very least she would have learnt what actually happened to the manuscripts after the reader had passed judgement on them. It would have been so very simple. "What a lot of work you have to do!" she could have exclaimed as they told her the procedure. But it was too late now. Her haste and panic had resulted in her learning nothing.

She walked home along the narrowest of the side streets, suddenly afraid that Laurence, taking what would admittedly be a very odd route from his office in Whitehall to Henrietta Street, Covent Garden, might drive past in a hansom cab and notice her and wonder what on earth she was doing in the area. By the time she reached Russell Square she was so sick of her own self-reproach and anxiety that she had managed to convince herself that the manuscript was most likely in the desk of one of the other clerks, awaiting a covering letter to be written to herself. It might even have been written already; the package might be waiting to go to post, or perhaps it was already in the post. She should have asked the boy to check that for her, of course. In fact, had it occurred to her before, she could have gone straight to the Post Office to see if there was a parcel there addressed to Miss Faith Freeman.

She stood at the corner of the square for a moment, half inclined to go back and do this now. It was one way of putting her mind completely at rest. But it was quite a long way to go, even if she took a cab, and she was thoroughly hot and tired and cross and sick to death of the wretched manuscript. As far as literary composition was concerned, her whole heart was now involved in the new novel—*The Price She Paid*—and the manuscript of *A Most Mysterious Death* could be at the bottom of the Thames for all she cared. In fact, had she been able to collect it from the publisher's office, she would very likely have dropped it over Waterloo Bridge in order to get rid of it for ever.

In the very moment when she said this to herself, she actually had a vision of the heroine of her new book in the very act of destroying what she had written. Jessie stood still on the pavement, gripping her parasol with both hands, her lips slightly parted, her eyes staring at nothing that was in front of them. Of course. That was the very next scene in the book. Love had temporarily triumphed; her heroine, in a desperate attempt to put her own ambitions aside and humbly love and admire the hero, would destroy her own work. Ah! What a scene that would make! It crowded in upon her with all its force and passion of renunciation. She could not wait another minute to see it taking shape under her pen.

Jessie hastened across the road, calculating how she could gain time and opportunity to write this scene. The headache might suffice a few more hours; it had, after all, been rather unwise to go out into the hot sun when she felt so unwell. If only she could slip up to her room unseen by any member of the household. If only she were her own mistress, accountable to nobody, and had her own home where she might do as she pleased. The humblest little cottage, the cheapest and dreariest lodgings, anything would do. She cared nothing for external appearances and did not even notice heat or cold or hunger or weariness or any other physical hardship when the fever of creation was upon her. But when it was over she felt very differently. She had grown to like living in comfortable houses, she who had been brought up so Spartanly, and she loved to wear good quality, though plain, dresses after the harsh uniform of the orphanage. She wanted her own beauty to be recognized and admired; she enjoyed the sense of power that it gave her. It was as if she were two different people. On the one side was the poor orphan girl who had made good as a governess and won the love of a man who could give her everything her heart desired; and on the other side was this strange, demon-possessed creature with the teeming imagination, who cared nothing whatsoever for anybody or anything, so long as there was paper and ink and freedom from interruption. There seemed to be no way of bringing the two to terms with each other, and the charmingly composed lady could turn into the fanatical writer at any moment and almost without warning.

Jessie had to wait for the parlourmaid to open the door because in her anxious departure from the house she had forgotten to take her key. When the girl opened the door Jessie did not, as she would normally do, smile and say "Thank you, Mary," but simply walked past the girl and straight up the stairs without a look or a word, for all the world, as Mary explained over and over again afterwards, as if she was in her sleep or going to her execution. Clara, coming upstairs a little later to find out whether or not Miss Brown wanted anything to eat and whether Miss Betty was to have any lessons that afternoon or to go for her usual walk, found that Miss Brown had locked herself into her room. Neither the door opening on to the second floor landing, nor that connecting with the now empty bedroom that had once been Mrs. Mackay's, opened to Clara's touch, and when she called out in some alarm to ask whether Miss Brown was all right, she received at first no reply, and then a very impatient: "Of course I am. I am resting, trying to sleep."

"Now I wonder what can have upset her," said Mrs. Greenaway when Clara reported this news. "This is how it was after Mrs. Mackay died. She would see and speak to nobody."

"Perhaps she had told Mr. Mackay that she cannot marry him," suggested the nursemaid.

"Perhaps she has," said the housekeeper. "I wish to goodness she would make up her mind one way or the other," she added, as she began to prepare a tray with the

child's meal. "It doesn't do any of us any good, this un-
certainty. And the poor little mite will have to miss her
lessons and eat all by herself again."

Clara had never known Mrs. Greenaway to speak so
sharply, and more was to come.

"She's putting on airs as if she was already mistress of
the household," said the housekeeper. "Supposing I was
to shut myself up in my room and neglect my duties! The
master would soon want to know the reason why, and if I
could give no good reason then I should be dismissed. But
not Miss Brown. Oh no, not Miss Brown. How long is it
going to go on, that's what I should like to know."

Mrs. Greenaway stood by the side of the big scrubbed
deal kitchen table, puffing slightly and waving a wooden
spoon in her indignation. Clara cut a slice of apple tart
and placed it on the child's tray.

"No!" exclaimed Mrs. Greenaway dramatically point-
ing the spoon at Clara. "Put that back. Go and fetch Miss
Betty. She shall eat with us, that she shall. And she can
stay here and talk to Cheepy—you will sing for her, won't
you, my pet?" Mrs. Greenaway crooked her finger and
made encouraging little noises at the canary, whose cage
had been brought in to stand by the kitchen window. "Go
on, Clara. Go and fetch the child. The master won't be
home yet. He need never know. And I don't care if he
does," she concluded defiantly, and kept up her muttering
about the poor little motherless mite even after Clara had
left the room.

The other maids and even the taciturn manservant Benson entered willingly into Mrs. Greenaway's scheme to
cheer up little Betty, and thus it was that Laurence Mackay
was able to come into the house, unseen and unheard, at
a much earlier hour than usual. There was no sign of any
of the servants in the upper part of the house; sounds of
laughter were coming up the stairs from the basement; and
in the study, the glass doors of the cabinet which housed
some of the smaller items of the collection stood open and

a duster lay on a shelf between a native cooking utensil and a vicious-looking little dagger. Benson had stopped in the midst of his cleaning work to obey the summons to eat.

Mr. Mackay did not even notice the slight disorder. If Miss Brown had come into the house like a sleepwalker, he came in like one in a nightmare. His face was grey, the lines were deep furrows, and a muscle at the corner of the mouth kept up a persistent involuntary twitching, giving an uncanny effect as if a death mask had come into spasmodic life. He dropped his hat on to the desk, sat down in the leather-covered chair behind it, and drew out from his case a thick bundle of handwritten sheets of paper. He laid them on the desk in front of him and began to read from the very beginning. The muscle in the face continued its twitching and the hands were held rigidly against the sides of the manuscript except when they made the slight motion of turning a page.

At one point there was a knock on the door and the square weather-beaten face of Benson appeared. The man at the desk murmured, "Not now" without looking up, and the manservant withdrew.

"Deep in his studies again," he told the assembled company in the housekeeper's room in the basement. "Wouldn't notice if the house were on fire." The housekeeper and the maids were playing a simple round game of cards with the child. "Come on, come on, it's your turn, Clara!" cried Betty, when Benson had finished speaking. Clara and the others returned to the game. They felt guilty and nervous about neglecting their duties in this manner. None of them had ever done such a thing before, but there was something strange, almost bewitched about the house this afternoon. They feared to go up into the sombre empty rooms more than they feared the master's wrath. They huddled together in the friendly warmth of each other's company, and Betty, triumphantly producing an ace of spades, squealed with delight.

Mr. Mackay read for a long time, making no movement other than the involuntary twitching of the muscle and the steady turning of the pages, but when the pile of pages remaining to be read had diminished to about one quarter of those lying on the other pile, a big change came over him. The mouth began to move in more violent spasms as he read page after page, until the whole face was working uncontrollably; the hands trembled so much that they could no longer place the sheets in a neat pile, but scattered them anyhow as soon as they were read. The last sentence of the manuscript ran as follows:

And now we must take our leave of Julia and her faithful Ernest who has held her in his heart with loyal and silent devotion for so long and is now to have his reward; we leave them on the deck of this great ocean-going steamer, facing the future in an unknown land with courage and determination, strong and secure in their love for each other; and Julia will never regret her choice, although perhaps now and then, when she gazes out at the wild prairies or treads the crowded pavements of the raw new city, she will spare a thought for that unhappy man who first taught her how to love, and will hope that God has brought some consolation into the darkness of his days.

After this there was written, in the centre of the page and in an elaborately decorated script as if the writer had lingered lovingly over the conclusion of the work and was reluctant to bid it farewell, the two words: "The End." Mr. Mackay stared at these words and at the last sentence for some minutes, his whole body trembling, his face contorted with pain and fury; then the fingers moved convulsively and tore the page across, and his head fell forward and rested on the desk. The muscles of face and fingers were still at last, while the raging pain continued its destructive work within his heart and mind.

A few minutes later, on the second storey of the house, Jessie Brown laid down her pen and read with a little smile of satisfaction the last few sentences she had written. It was going to be all right. The great scene of the heroine destroying her own work had taken the shape she had desired. It was powerful; it was convincing; Chapman's reader was going to like that, she felt sure. She yawned, stretched her cramped fingers, closed the notebook in which she had been writing, locked it in the drawer and slipped the key into the usual hiding place. Then she gave herself a little shake, smoothed down her dress and her hair, looked into the mirror at the image of the calm, serene governess, and suddenly became aware that she was excessively hungry.

"Good heavens!" she exclaimed. "How can it possibly be so late? It is like magic, like a dream. It seems barely a second since I began to write and yet I have lived through a whole age of my characters' thoughts and emotions. The mind knows no time, acknowledges no limits of place. How wonderful a faculty is this imagination! And how frightening!"

She unbolted the door of her room and paused for a moment on the second-floor landing. The house seemed uncannily quiet. Where were all the maids? It was strange that none of them had approached her room again. And where was Betty? She was the least noisy of children, but nevertheless there was usually some sounds of movement or voices coming from the nursery. Slowly Jessie descended the stairs, one hand lightly touching the smooth polished wood of the banister, the other holding the skirt of her lilac dress that stood out light and plain against the deep reds and blues of the stair carpet.

She looked into the nursery and saw nobody there; the same with the child's bedroom, the bathroom, the ironing and workroom. Becoming somewhat alarmed now, she made her way down to the front hall. The door of the big drawing-room was closed, the doors of the dining-room and of the study were closed, and so too was the door at the head of the stairs leading to the basement. This was unusual, indeed unprecedented. With all the carrying up and down of trays and hot water and slops that went on in even such a quietly run household as this, it was essential that there should always be free access between the working part of the house and the rest. Jessie's unease increased. What on earth had happened during that long moment when she had been transported into another world—a world of her own creation! Was the Creator of the Universe, was Time itself, playing tricks? Had she also been transported into next week? next month? next year?

She shook herself impatiently and took a grip on her thoughts. There was quite enough to worry about already without adding to it such alarming metaphysical speculations. First and foremost, there was this business about her earlier manuscript and about Laurence visiting the offices of Chapman and Hall. She would need every bit of her strength and presence of mind to talk to him about his interview and find out what exactly had happened without in the least giving herself away. Then she was going to have to make frequent visits to the Poste Restante counter at the main Post Office until she received a reply to her appeal to Mr. Meredith. And then summon up her strength for that interview in which she would lay the full truth before him. And meanwhile she would have to find some way of keeping Laurence happy without fully committing herself; and she simply must attend to Betty and her own duties in this household, which she had been neglecting disgracefully. At this rate the servants would be taking everything into their own hands and practically running the place. In fact it looked as if they were doing so already, shutting themselves up in the basement like this.

Jessie took a deep breath and made a resolution. She would concentrate now on regaining her grasp on the household and on keeping Laurence happy. The writing would have to be done mainly at night. After all, that was how *A Most Mysterious Death* had been written. She had been indulging herself most imprudently these last two days and it would have to stop. In any case, *The Price She Paid* was now so firmly striding along its way that she no longer feared to lose the inspiration if the writing of it had to be postponed for several hours after the idea of a scene had formed itself in her mind.

She stretched a hand out to the door at the top of the basement stairs, intending to do down and announce that she was feeling better now and very hungry, at the same time taking stock of the position with a view to tactfully taking the reins of government into her own hands again. As her fingers grasped the handle she heard the sound of voices coming from below, and at the same moment there came to her ears another sound, a little click as of a hard object falling on to a hard surface. There was nothing alarming about the sound in itself, but Jessie was startled because it had seemed to come from behind her, from the direction of the study. Was Laurence there? She had not noticed his hat on the stand in the hall where he always placed it when he came into the house. Could it perhaps be some intruder who had gained access over the wall of the small garden at the rear of the house, and broken through the conservatory and into the study? She had better investigate: it would be dreadful if anything were to be stolen from Laurence's collection—he would be so upset. And if Laurence himself were there, then it would be as well to get the meeting over and know the worst at once.

She knocked on the door. There was no reply. After putting her ear to the keyhole and hearing no further sound she turned the handle and pushed the door open.

16

"Passions Spin the Plot"

Laurence was in the act of straightening up after picking up something from the end of the hearth next to which stood the glass-fronted cabinet. As Jessie came into the room he moved towards the desk and she saw the glint of something pale on his hand. He placed the object on the desk and she saw that it was one of the little ivory daggers that were kept in the cabinet. Her first fleeting thought, before her eyes had taken in anything else about the room and its owner, was that he was going to use the dagger to slit some papers, or to cut the pages of a new book. She stood just inside the door and her eyes moved from where the sharp little ivory weapon lay, along the desk to a pile of sheets of paper and some scattered pages lying around it. She stepped forward to take a closer look. The handwriting came into focus; the torn last page, with the elaborately written words "The End" now right at the edge of one of the fragments, came at her with a sickening shock of realization. She raised her hands to her throat and gave a little gasp. Then she looked up and saw his face and the gasp turned into a muffled scream.

"Laurence! Forgive me!" Her hands were clasped together now, beseechingly, and she spoke in a quick low voice. "I know you did not kill Louisa—neither in that manner nor in any other. I know it is not true. But we talked of it—it was in both our minds. It could have happened that way—it fitted in so well with the story. I could not resist it. But I *know* you are not guilty! I know it! And the book will never be published. It will never come to any other eyes. I swear to you that no one else will ever see it.''

''But can you swear that no one but ourselves has read it?''

His voice was harsh and strained, as if he was controlling himself only with a tremendous effort. He still looked grimmer than Jessie had ever known him look, but she relaxed just a trifle. Laurence was often harsh and grim. She had learnt how to handle him in this mood and evoke his softer side, and she would manage it yet again, in this her greatest trial.

''It is not so bad as you fear, my dearest,'' she said putting all the loving sweetness that she could possibly summon up into her voice. ''I will explain it all and then I will beg you to forgive me.''

''Yes. You will explain.''

He stood facing her, gripping the side of the desk with both hands. She drew up a chair to the other side of the desk and sat down before she spoke again. The dagger and the manuscript lay on the polished mahogany surface between them.

''I began to write,'' she said, ''because I felt so guilty after Louisa's death. I felt I had betrayed her. It eased me to tell the story. And then it gripped me, the writing itself. It took complete possession of me. Oh, I cannot explain that! It was a madness—a delirium. I could not control it.''

''And in your madness and your delirium you took the manuscript to a well-known firm of publishers and offered it to them for publication—for the whole world to read.''

His voice was dangerously calm now. Jessie, intent upon her own act, was relieved by the calm and did not notice the danger.

"I never really intended that it should be published," she said. "You must believe me! You must indeed. I only wanted an opinion. I believed that I could write. I wanted to know whether another reader would agree with me."

"Then why did you not show your manuscript to me?"

"Because—because." She faltered for the first time. "Because it was so obvious that the story was about us— because I had pictured you as a murderer—" She broke off as the enormity of what she was saying hit her in all its full force for the first time. "Oh my God, what have I done? Oh Laurence, my dearest, forgive me, forgive me!" She stretched out her hands to him across the desk, face upturned, eyes brimming over. "Forgive me. For God's sake forgive me."

"You have not answered my question," he said stiffly, completely ignoring her pleading looks and gestures. "I asked who else has read this?"

"To my knowledge, only Chapman's reader," she replied, speaking in a very low voice and letting her hands fall into her lap again and turning her face away.

"And what was the opinion of Chapman's reader?"

"Very favourable." Her voice was now almost inaudible. "He thinks I am a born writer."

He made no response and for several minutes there was silence. The woman stared at her hands, now clasped together and resting lightly on the side of the desk; the man stared at his, gripping with great force the other side.

"But it will not be published," murmured Jessie at last. "I have written to say I am withdrawing it from offer. I am bitterly sorry to cause you such distress. I wish with all my heart that you had never had to know about this. The manuscript will be destroyed now. No one else will ever see it. It has been seen only by one pair of eyes other than our own, and those are of someone of the highest integrity—we can count on his discretion."

"Indeed? Why then was the manuscript lying on the Managing Director's desk for every tuppeny-ha'penny

clerk to see? Every casual visitor to the office? How can
you talk of discretion when I myself found it only too
fatally easy first of all to read and then to remove the
manuscript?''

''You actually took it off Mr. Chapman's desk?''

She looked up at him then, in great surprise. That Laurence, whom she had always regarded as above all petty
deceits and underhand dealing, should actually descend to
reading something that did not concern him and then ab-
sconding with it, was altogether astonishing to her. But
how else could he have come by it, she told herself, trying
to take a firmer grip on her scattered wits, except by
stealth? Mr. Chapman would certainly not have handed it
to him. Truly the ways of a man deeply in love were very
strange.

''I am sure that no one will ever believe that you are
capable of murder,'' she said hesitantly, at the same time
thinking to herself: But he is capable of theft—have I perhaps misjudged his character after all? Or was I perhaps
right after all that he is capable of murder?

''I do not care whether they believe me capable of murder or not!'' he cried, and for the first time some of the
repressed passion showed itself in his voice. ''Let them
believe it! They may well be right. I could have killed
Louisa. I do not deny it. It was in my mind. I could have
killed that poor, frightened, innocent creature. And for
whose sake? For yours, yours, yours! You who swore you
loved me—you who have deceived me!''

She got up from her chair and backed against the desk
as he came round it towards her. She held out her hands
as if to protect herself and cried, ''Laurence—forgive me,
I entreat you! I have deceived you, I confess. I have written this novel without your knowing. It has meant so much
to me. It has sometimes taken the place in my heart that
you alone should hold. I confess it. I am guilty. I can only
plead that it gripped me like a passion—like a passion of
love. And I could not resist it.''

"Like a passion of love!" he repeated, all the long repressed violence breaking out at last, the worse for having been kept so long in check. "Like a passion of love! Who is he? Who is the man?"

"The man? What man?"

She looked up at him in complete bewilderment, frowning slightly, her outstretched arms falling to her sides.

"The man. Ernest in the story. Your lover. The man with whom you have been deceiving me. The man who has been first in your heart for years, although so far away. The man with whom you are planning to elope, start a new life in the New World together."

"Oh my God! Oh no, no, no!"

She closed her eyes and let out a long shuddering breath as the reason for his fury and the nature of his misconception at last dawned on her.

"Listen, Laurence," she cried, gaining some control over herself again. "There is no Ernest. There is no man. It is all imagination. The ending is all made up. I did not know how to finish the story, so I invented an ending with a long-lost lover."

This served only to infuriate him further. He stepped forward and caught hold of her arms. "Who is the man? What is his name?" he repeated, beside himself with passion.

"God help me, what am I to do," murmured Jessie to herself, becoming really desperate now. Never for one moment had she imagined that events could take such a turn. Laurence's fury at being depicted as a murderer in her novel she had expected; that he should believe her ending, her feeble, tacked-on ending, and conclude from it that she was deceiving him with another lover—why, this was beyond anything. It simply could not be true. Yet the force of his grip and the intense passion of jealousy in his voice were only too alarmingly true. He is going to kill me, she thought. Good God, is it come to this, that I am to die for a fiction? For a moment or two terror and revulsion overcame her, and then she summoned up all her strength and all her brains for one last effort.

"There is no Ernest, there is no other man," she said again as steadily and calmly as she was able. "The end of the novel is the weak part—a weak invention. I was to alter the ending because it did not read convincingly enough. Mr. Meredith said so. He said he could not believe in the end."

Suddenly inspiration came to her.

"If you cannot believe me, Laurence, then ask Mr. Meredith. He knows what is true or could have been true and he knows what is simply false. He will tell you! He knows that there is no Ernest—there is no true end."

For a moment she had a flicker of hope. The grip that was nearly paralysing her arms did not relax but she thought she saw the faintest shadow of doubt on his face. If I can but hold him at bay, she thought, until I can lay my fingers on that dagger. It must be somewhere near—I saw it at this end of the desk. I do not mean to hurt him— only to defend myself.

With the less tortured of her arms she felt behind her while she looked full into his face and said: "Let me go now, Laurence. Stay but to ask this question and then do with me what you will. Ask Mr. Meredith. He will tell you that this is no true ending."

"A poet!" he cried contemptuously. "Poets are dreamers."

"But they often dream the truth."

The little flicker of hope remained. She believed that he had listened to her, even in the midst of his uncontrollable jealous rage, and she continued to argue and to plead while all the time her fingers felt behind her for the dagger.

17

A Poet Arrives Too Late

"What d'you think will happen, George?" asked Frederic Chapman as the hansom cab made its infuriatingly slow way through the crowded London streets, constantly held up by slower-moving vehicles in front or by lumbering drays coming out of side turnings.

"God knows," said Mr. Meredith gloomily, as he tried to peer around a four-wheeler that was currently blocking their way. "I could walk quicker than this."

"You could, but I couldn't," said Mr. Chapman, holding his companion by the arm as if fearful that he might be left to deal with this crisis alone. "You are to stay here with me."

"What sort of a man is he?" asked Mr. Meredith when the horse was trotting once again.

"Mackay? Odd sort of fellow. Bit inhuman, I thought," said Mr. Chapman, and described in detail how his own feelings about the visitor had changed during the course of the interview.

"That would be after he had managed to read enough to take in the gist of the manuscript and to guess at its authorship," said Mr. Meredith. "It is hardly surprising that he was not particularly interested in his own book at that moment."

"No," agreed Mr. Chapman rather shamefacedly. It

was damned generous of George, he was saying to himself, to refrain from rubbing in the fact that none of this would have happened if he had not left the visitor alone in his office for so long. Frederic Chapman had been prepared for some nasty comments about this, and he felt he would have deserved them, but nothing had been said. George had grasped the whole thing in a flash and really had turned up trumps, without wasting time on any reproaches.

"Did you get the impression that he might be a violent sort of man, Fred?" he asked now.

"I would not be surprised. These tight buttoned-up fellows often are when roused. And the author, who after all must know him very well, did depict him as a murderer."

"Yes, but I should not take too much notice of that."

"You mean she might have made it up?" Frederic Chapman looked rather taken aback. "In that case what is all this panic about?"

"She might and she might not. It doesn't really matter."

"Doesn't matter? But my dear fellow, surely that is the nub of the whole thing? Are we not rushing off to try to save this young woman from the possible consequences of her rashness in revealing the fact that she knows this man to be a murderer?"

"Partly," replied Mr. Meredith, "but also partly something even worse."

"Worse!" Mr. Chapman looked outraged. "What ever could be worse? If there are worse crimes than murder I do not know of them."

"To a man deeply in love there is an even worse crime."

"For God's sake, George, do not speak in riddles now!" cried Mr. Chapman. "Tell me what you are thinking in straight language, there's a good fellow. I cannot endure to puzzle my brain just now."

Mr. Meredith told him exactly what he was thinking, in

the straightest possible language, and Mr. Chapman leant back against the seat of the cab and groaned.

"But it is such a silly feeble sort of ending," he said. "Everyone must see that. Nobody could possibly be convinced of its truth."

"Nobody except perhaps a jealous lover," observed his companion.

Frederic Chapman groaned again. "You are right as usual, George. We are thinking of literary judgements, are we not?"

"A mind half crazed with jealous suspicions would see no such subtleties," was the uncomforting reply.

"So he may well believe that she—?" Mr. Chapman could not finish the question.

"Exactly," said Mr. Meredith.

"But there may really be another lover."

"There may be. That scarcely makes the situation any less explosive."

"If only we had never seen the wretched book in the first place," said Mr. Chapman with deep feeling.

"You cannot wish it more than I," retorted Mr. Meredith in equally heartfelt tones. "I can only be thankful that the great majority of manuscripts are not of this nature."

Talking in this way, the two very worried-looking gentlemen from a well-known publishing house at last found themselves pulling up at the front door of Number Twenty-two Russell Square. It looked just an ordinary town mansion, much like any other. There was nothing in its external appearance to suggest that a drama of life and death was taking place within.

"I only hope to heaven we are not making utter fools of ourselves," said Mr. Chapman as he tugged at the bell-rope.

"A manuscript has disappeared from your desk," Mr. Meredith reminded him. "We have every right to enquire

of Mr. Mackay whether he took it away by mistake among
his other papers when he left your office.''

"I suppose so," said Mr. Chapman uneasily. "You do
the talking, George."

"All right. Ssh. Someone is coming."

The door was being opened, rather slowly and awk-
wardly, as if the person on the other side was having difficulty with the latch. Automatically the two men braced
themselves, preparing to talk to a maidservant or a manservant in a firm yet conciliatory manner. The door was
flung wide at last but it was no servant who stood there.
A tall young woman in a pale lilac dress clung to the door
handle as if that alone was keeping her upright. Her eyes
were wild and terrified, her black hair falling over her face
in limp strands, and on the front of her dress, near to the
heart, there was a deep red stain. She looked first at Mr.
Chapman and then her eyes turned to his companion. A
glint of recognition came into her eyes and then a harsh
sound came from her lips that might have been laughter;
but there was no gaiety in it; it was a laugh that chilled
the blood.

"Too late!" she cried. "You've come too late to tell
him the truth!"

And with a swift and unexpected movement she let go
of the door-handle and dashed between them, so that in-
voluntarily they stepped back and made way for her as she
ran down the steps and away round the square. Mr. Chapman stared after her, open-mouthed. Mr. Meredith made
a movement as if to follow her and then paused to say,
"If she is injured . . ." He did not finish the sentence. A
whole train of servants had appeared from the back of the
hall, and a young girl in parlourmaid's uniform was the
first to reach the front door. She took hold of the handle
that the fugitive had been grasping and looked up at the
visitors in nervous enquiry.

"We have called to see Mr. Mackay," said Mr. Meredith, producing a card. "If you would be good enough to hand this to him."

The girl let go of the door-handle, took the card, and let out a little scream. On her fingers, and now on the white piece of pasteboard, was clearly visible a dark red stain. She held her hand and the card away from her, staring at them in alarm. The two visiting gentlemen and the three women servants stared likewise.

"Where is Miss Brown?" asked the oldest of the three women at last.

"In a lilac dress?" It was Mr. Meredith who spoke.

"Yes, sir."

"She has just run out of the house. She was grasping the door-handle. One of you had better go after her." He looked at the short, sturdy manservant who had now joined the others.

"Yes, sir," said Benson, and hurried out of the house.

"Where is Mr. Mackay's room?" Mr. Chapman decided that it was time for him to take command.

"This way, sir." Mrs. Greenaway led the way to the door of the study. It was standing ajar. She stood barring the way into the room. "If you will kindly wait in the hall, please, gentlemen. Mr. Mackay does not like to be disturbed when he is reading or writing, but I will ask him if he is free to see you now. What did you say the names were?"

Fresh cards were produced; the bloodstained one had fallen to the floor where the shrinking parlourmaid had dropped it.

"Cannot think what can be the matter with Miss Brown," muttered Mrs. Greenaway. "Excuse me, gentlemen, we are all at sixes and sevens today. I will see if Mr. Mackay is at liberty to see you."

Her belated attempt at keeping up appearances lasted only for a moment. She took three steps into the study and the next moment those crowding outside the door heard a piercing shriek. Clara and the housemaid, following her,

added their screams to hers. Mr. Chapman turned to the
trembling parlourmaid, Mary, who was still trying to rub
the bloodstain off her fingers, and said, with that kindness
and gentleness that was so unexpected a characteristic of
this bluff and autocratic man: "I think you had better run
and fetch the police, my dear. Can you do that?"

"Yes, sir."

"You know where to go?"

"Yes, sir. My Jimmy—my young man, sir, he is a po-
liceman."

"Good. Just a minute, though. Is there anybody else in
the house?"

"Only Miss Betty, sir. Oh dear. She is all alone downstairs. I must go to her."

"No, you run off and get the police. Tell them it is a
case of murder or attempted murder. I will send one of
the others to look after Miss Betty."

Five minutes later Mr. Chapman was as much in charge
of the distracted household as ever he had been of his
publishing firm. Ever a man of action, he was at his best
when there was something positive to be done and he was
no longer chasing ghosts and will-o'-the-wisps. Clara was
despatched to attend to the child, the housemaid was sent
to prepare the front room for the reception of the police
inspector, and Mrs. Greenaway, alternately soothed and
bullied into comparative equanimity, stood next to Mr.
Chapman in the master's study, carefully averting her eyes
from her master. Laurence Mackay lay slumped against
the side of the desk, his head lolling forward, the ivory
handle of a dagger protruding from his breast, his clothes
spattered with bloodstains. Mr. Meredith, his face twisted
up in pity and distress, was leaning over the scattered pages
of the manuscript of *A Most Mysterious Death*.

"It is as we feared, Fred," he said.

"What is?" asked Mr. Chapman.

"He must have believed the ending. See how the last
page is torn in two. The rest lie neatly—even those dealing

with the murder. It was not that that drove him to despair. It was the end—the feeble, lying end.'' He shook his head and his face twisted up again as if he had drunk from a very bitter cup. ''Too cruel. Could she not convince him that she had invented the end?''

Mr. Chapman studied the scattered pages in his turn. ''I believe that is it, George,'' he said slowly, and he too looked as if he had bitten on something very sour. ''Though how on earth we are to tell this to the police . . .''

Mrs. Greenaway, who had been looking in bewilderment from one to the other, intervened at this point. ''Excuse me, gentlemen,'' she said, ''but are either of you by any chance acquainted with Mr. Mackay?''

''Only with his *alter ego*,'' said Mr. Meredith, earning an even more puzzled look from the housekeeper while Mr. Chapman made a not very successful attempt to explain.

''Mr. Mackay steal a manuscript!'' she cried indignantly, holding on to the only part of his statement that she could understand. ''He would never do such a thing! He is—he was—a gentleman of the strictest honour.''

The two men exchanged hopeless glances. There seemed little point in worrying the poor shocked housekeeper any more with their fantastic tale. The inspector of police was a different matter. He was youngish and shrewd-looking, and he listened with keen attention to the extraordinary story told by the two gentlemen from the publishing firm.

''If I take your meaning rightly, sir,'' he said to Mr. Chapman who had completed the narrative, ''that the deceased gentleman believed he had learnt from this manuscript that the woman he loved was deceiving him with another man, then that would be reason enough for him to kill her perhaps, but not for her to kill him. It is the man who lies there stabbed to death, not the woman. How do you account for that?''

Self-defence, was all the suggestion they had to offer.

"No doubt she will enter a plea of self-defence at her trial," said the police inspector.

Mr. Chapman and Mr. Meredith once more exchanged unhappy looks. Benson had brought back the news that the fugitive had eluded him somewhere in the maze of small streets between the Strand and the riverside, but a police search had been set in motion and it was hardly to be supposed that she could get away, conspicuous as she was, with no money, and perhaps even suffering from an injury, although Benson declared it as his opinion that she could not be hurt, she ran so fast, and the bloodstains they had seen on her dress and her hands must have come from the dead man and not from herself.

"Has she friends with whom she might hide?" the police inspector asked Mrs. Greenaway.

The housekeeper knew of none. In fact neither she nor any of the other servants knew anything about Miss Brown at all apart from her position in the household. Certainly they had not the slightest idea that she had written a novel. As regards her relationship with Mr. Mackay, the supposition that she had refused his offer of marriage was repeated *ad nauseam*, but this offer, as the inspector very reasonably said, was hardly a reason for her to stab him to death; all she needed to do was to seek another post.

"It is a case of passion if ever I saw one," he said.

"With the roles of murderer and victim reversed," put in Mr. Meredith. The inspector gave him a none too friendly glance: he had been working up, with some complacency, to make this very remark himself. He asked a few more questions and made a few more comments, determined to show that he was a man of wisdom and experience who could keep his end up even with supercilious gentlemen from publishing houses, and then he let them go, with the warning that they would certainly be called upon to give evidence at a murder trial.

"It is worse than we could possibly have imagined," said Mr. Chapman when he and Mr. Meredith were once again alone together. "Terrible, terrible. What d'you suppose really happened?"

"He tried to kill her, I suppose, and she hit at him first."

There was silence for a minute or two, and then Mr. Chapman said: "You know, George, I cannot help feeling most dreadfully guilty about it all."

"So do I," said Mr. Meredith.

"And yet again I really do not see that it is our fault, any more than it is Laurence Mackay's fault, or even the girl's own fault, come to that."

" 'In tragic life'," murmured Mr. Meredith, " 'no villain need be, passions spin the plot.' "

"What's that you are saying, George?"

"I said that nobody is to blame. Nothing but human nature itself."

"True. Very true."

Again there was a silence.

"I can't help hoping she will get away," Mr. Chapman said at last.

"So do I, Fred, but I cannot see that it is possible."

"To think that we shall be obliged to bear witness against her and perhaps even send her to execution!"

"Not against her," corrected Mr. Meredith. "The whole tenor of what we have to say points to her having acted in self-defence. Nevertheless I too find the prospect intensely distasteful."

But as it turned out, neither of the two gentlemen from the firm of publishers was called upon to enter the witness-box at the trial of Jessie Brown for the murder of Laurence Mackay, for it never took place. In the small hours of the following day a night watchman tramping round the wharves near to the southern end of Waterloo Bridge noticed something pale floating in the dirty water, caught up at the side of a raft. A little later the body of a woman clothed in a lilac-coloured dress was taken out of the Thames. There was no evidence to show how she had come there, but when the body was identified, the presumption of suicide seemed a fairly reasonable one. Only the previous week some wretched girl deserted by her lover had jumped off Waterloo Bridge and drowned herself.

The news was brought to Frederic Chapman while the Saturday cricket match at Banstead was in full swing. He had been taking very little pleasure in the occasion: his guests had never known old Fred to be such an absent-minded, glum-looking host.

"I wonder if George knows yet," he said to his wife. "I think I will drive over to Box Hill and tell him."

"Yes, my dear, that will do you good," she replied. "You will feel much better after you have talked it over with Mr. Meredith, and I will make some excuse for your absence."

Mr. Chapman did feel better. Mr. Meredith had not yet heard about the death of the lady in black, but he had received through the post, together with some other papers from the office, a letter from her, which he produced. It had that peculiar poignancy that always clings to the living thoughts of someone recently dead. The two men looked at it together.

" 'I appeal to you not as a woman, but as a writer'," read Mr. Chapman aloud. "My dear George, my dear old friend, how very distressing to receive this now."

Mr. Chapman's old friend did indeed look more upset than Mr. Chapman had ever known him. His face was bleak and grey. They talked for a while in the pleasant little sitting-room with the window looking out on cherry trees and the green hillside, and then Mr. Meredith made a ghastly attempt at a joke.

"Well, Fred, you can publish your best-seller now if you wish. You still have the copy."

"I would rather the firm go bankrupt than touch that book again," said Frederic Chapman with great feeling. "Well, I must get back to my guests now. Try not to take it too much to heart, old chap."

After he had gone, Mr. Meredith sat for a long time perfectly still, staring into the empty fireplace, his back to the window that gave on to the sunny garden. But by the time Marie Meredith returned from a visit that she had been making with the children, he had recovered himself, and when later that evening he told her the full story it was in an aloof, detached sort of manner as if he was speaking of people who had nothing at all to do with him.

"She had the makings of a very fine writer," he concluded. "It is a loss to literature."

Marie Meredith was shocked and moved right out of her usual placidity. "It is terrible," she said with tears in her eyes. "Two lives in their prime—and all for a misunderstanding. It is truly tragic."

"It is a loss to literature," repeated George coolly.

Marie Meredith said no more. She had chosen her mate freely and for the most part was well content with her lot, but there were times when she could not help thinking that writers had no hearts.

Notes on Sources

The historical material for this novel was originally collected for a dissertation on Victorian Publishers' Readers
submitted to the University of Sussex for the MA degree
in 1975. Among authorities consulted were:

AUTHOR WAUGH: *One Hundred Years of Publishing*.
  Chapman and Hall, 1930.

B. W. MATZ: "George Meredith as Publisher's
  Reader." *Fortnightly Review*, August, 1919.

DIANE JOHNSON: *The True History of the First Mrs.
  Meredith and Other Lesser Lives*. Heinemann, 1972.

LADY BUTCHER: *Memories of George Meredith O.M.*
  Chapman and Hall, 1919.

R. E. SENCOURT: *The Life of George Meredith*. Chapman and Hall, 1929.

LIONEL STEVENSON: *The Ordeal of George Meredith*.
  Peter Owen, 1954.

GILLIAN BEER: *Meredith: a Change of Masks*. Athlone
  Press, 1970.

FLORENCE HARDY: *The Early Life of Thomas Hardy*.
  Macmillan, 1925.

The Letters of George Gissing to his Family. Constable,
  1931.

S. C. CRONWRIGHT-SCHREINER: *The Life of Olive
  Schreiner*. Haskell House, New York, 1973.

DORIS LANGLEY MOORE: *The Life of E. Nesbit*. Benn, 1967.

CHRISTOPHER DERRICK: *Reader's Report on the Writing of Novels*. Gollancz, 1969.

The Dictionary of National Biography.

The Girls' Own Paper for the 1880s.

I have also been helped by fellow students and other kind friends.